published by Kodansha International Ltd.

House of The Sleeping Beauties

and other stories

by Yasunari Kawabata

with an introduction by
Yukio Mishima

translated by Edward G. Seidensticker

Distributed in Continental Europe by Boxerbooks, Inc., Zurich;
and in the Far East by Japan Publications Trading Co., C.P.O.
Box 722, Tokyo.
Published by Kodansha International Ltd., 2–12–21, Otowa,
Bunkyo-ku, Tokyo, Japan and Kodansha International/USA,
Ltd., 577 College Avenue, Palo Alto, California 94306.
Library of Congress Catalog Card No. 69-19272
SBN 87011–082–6
Second printing, 1969.

Contents

Introduction 7

House of the Sleeping Beauties 13

One Arm 103

Of Birds and Beasts 127

Introduction

There would seem to be, among the works of great writers, those that might be called of the obverse or the exterior, their meaning on the surface, and those of the reverse or interior, the meaning hidden behind; or we might liken them to exoteric and esoteric Buddhism. In the case of Mr. Kawabata, *Snow Country* falls in the former category, while "House of the Sleeping Beauties" is most certainly an esoteric masterpiece.

In an esoteric masterpiece, a writer's most secret, deeply hidden themes make their appearance. Such a work is dominated not by openness and clarity but by a strangling tightness. In place of limpidness and purity we have density; rather than the broad, open world we have a closed room. The spirit of the author, flinging away all inhibitions, shows itself in its boldest form. I have elsewhere likened "House of the Sleeping Beauties" to a submarine in which people are trapped and the air is gradually disappearing. While in the grip of this story, the reader sweats and grows dizzy, and knows with the greatest immediacy the terror of lust urged on by the approach of death. Or, given a certain reading, the work might be likened to a film negative. A print made from it would no doubt show the whole of the day' light world in which we live, reveal the last detail of its bright, plastic hypocrisy.

"House of the Sleeping Beauties" is unusual among Mr. Kawa' bata's works for its formal perfection. At the end the dark girl dies, and "the woman of the house" says: "There is the other girl." With this last cruel remark, she brings down the house of lust, until then so carefully and minutely fabricated, in a collapse inhuman beyond description. It may appear to be accidental, but it is not. At a stroke it reveals the inhuman essence in a structure apparent' ly built with solidity and care—an essence shared by "the woman of the house" with old Eguchi himself.

And that is why old Eguchi "had never been more sharply struck by a remark."

Eroticism has not, for Mr. Kawabata, pointed to totality, for eroticism as totality carries within itself humanity. Lust inevi' tably attaches itself to fragments, and, quite without subjectivity, the sleeping beauties themselves are fragments of human beings, urging lust to its highest intensity. And, paradoxically, a beauti' ful corpse, from which the last traces of spirit have gone, gives rise to the strongest feelings of life. From the reflection of these violent feelings of the one who loves, the corpse sends forth the strongest radiance of life.

At a deeper level, this theme is related to another of importance in Mr. Kawabata's writing, his worship of virgins. This is the source of his clean lyricism, but below the surface it has something in common with the themes of death and impossibility. Because a virgin ceases to be a virgin once she is assaulted, impossibility of attainment is a necessary premise for putting virginity beyond agnosticism. And does not impossibility of attainment put eroticism and death forever at that same point? And if we novelists do not belong on the side of "life" (if we are confined to an abstraction of a kind of perpetual neutrality), then the "radiance of life" can only appear in the realm where death and eroticism are together.

"House of the Sleeping Beauties" begins with old Eguchi's visit to a secret house ruled over by "a small woman in her mid-forties." Since the reason for her presence is to make that extremely important remark at the conclusion, she is drawn with ominous detail, down to the large bird on her obi and the fact that she is left-handed.

One is struck with admiration at the precision, the extraordinary fineness of detail, with which Mr. Kawabata describes the first of the "sleeping beauties" the sixty-seven-year-old Eguchi spends the night with—as if she were being caressed by words alone. Of course it hints at a certain inhuman objectivity in the visual quality of male lust.

"Her right hand and wrist were at the edge of the quilt. Her left arm seemed to stretch diagonally under the quilt. Her right thumb was half hidden under her cheek. The fingers on the pillow beside her face were slightly curved in the softness of sleep, though not enough to erase the delicate hollows where they joined the hand. The warm redness was gradually richer from the palm to the fingertips. It was a smooth, glowing white hand."

"Her knee was slightly forward, leaving his legs in an awkward position. It took no inspection to tell him that she was not on the defensive, that she did not have her right knee resting on her left. The right knee was pulled back, the leg stretched out."

Thus the girl who has become a "living doll" is for the old man "life that can be touched with confidence."

And what a splendidly erotic technique we have when old Kiga sees the *aoki* berries in the garden. "Numbers of them lay on the ground. Kiga picked one up. Toying with it, he told Egu⁄ chi of the secret house." From this passage or near it, the feeling of confinement and suffocation begins to come over the reader. The usual techniques of dialogue and character description are of no use in "House of the Sleeping Beauties," for the girls are asleep. It must be very rare for literature to give so vividly a sense of individual life through descriptions of sleeping figures.

YUKIO MISHIMA

House of the
Sleeping Beauties

House of the Sleeping Beauties

I

He was not to do anything in bad taste, the woman of the inn warned old Eguchi. He was not to put his finger into the mouth of the sleeping girl, or try anything else of that sort.

There were this room, some four yards square, and the one next to it, but apparently no other rooms upstairs; and, since the downstairs seemed too restricted for guest rooms, the place could scarcely be called an inn at all. Probably because its secret allowed none, there was no sign at the gate. All was silence. Admitted through the locked gate, old Eguchi had seen only the woman to whom he was now talking. It was his first visit. He did not know whether she was the proprietress or a maid. It seemed best not to ask.

A small woman perhaps in her mid-forties, she had a youthful voice, and it was as if she had especially cultivated a calm, steady manner. The thin lips scarcely parted as she spoke. She did not often look at Eguchi. There was something in the dark eyes that lowered his defenses, and she seemed quite at ease herself. She made tea from the iron kettle on the bronze brazier. The tea leaves and the quality of the brewing were astonishingly good, for the place and the occasion—to put old Eguchi more at ease. In the alcove hung a painting by Kawai Gyokudō, probably a reproduction, of a mountain village warm with autumn leaves. Nothing suggested that the room had unusual secrets.

"And please don't try to wake her. Not that you could, whatever you did. She's sound asleep and knows nothing." The woman said it again: "She'll sleep on and on and know nothing at all, from start to finish. Not even who's been with her. You needn't worry."

Eguchi said nothing of the doubts that were coming over him.

"She's a very pretty girl. I only take guests I know I can trust."

As Eguchi looked away his eye fell to his wrist watch.

"What time is it?"

"A quarter to eleven."

"I should think so. Old gentlemen like to go to bed early and get up early. So whenever you're ready."

The woman got up and unlocked the door to the next room. She used her left hand. There was nothing remarkable about the act, but Eguchi held his breath as he watched her. She looked into the other room. She was no doubt used to looking through doorways, and there was nothing unusual about the back turned toward Eguchi. Yet it seemed strange. There was a large, strange bird on the knot of her obi. He did not know what species it might be. Why should such realistic eyes and feet have been put on a stylized bird? It was not that the bird was disquieting in itself, only that the design was bad; but if disquiet

☙ 14 ❧

was to be tied to the woman's back, it was there in the bird. The ground was a pale yellow, almost white.

The next room seemed to be dimly lighted. The woman closed the door without locking it, and put the key on the table before Eguchi. There was nothing in her manner to suggest that she had inspected a secret room, nor was there in the tone of her voice.

"Here is the key. I hope you sleep well. If you have trouble getting to sleep, you will find some sleeping medicine by the pillow."

"Have you anything to drink?"

"I don't keep spirits."

"I can't even have a drink to put myself to sleep?"

"No."

"She's in the next room?"

"She's asleep, waiting for you."

"Oh?" Eguchi was a little surprised. When had the girl come into the next room? How long had she been asleep? Had the woman opened the door to make sure that she was asleep? Eguchi had heard from an old acquaintance who frequented the place that a girl would be waiting, asleep, and that she would not awaken; but now that he was here he seemed unable to believe it.

"Where will you undress?" She seemed ready to help him. He was silent. "Listen to the waves. And the wind."

"Waves?"

"Good night." She left him.

Alone, old Eguchi looked around the room, bare and without contrivance. His eye came to rest on the door to the next room. It was of cedar, some three feet wide. It seemed to have been put in after the house was finished. The wall too, upon examination, seemed once to have been a sliding partition, now sealed over to make the secret chamber of the sleeping beauties. The color matched that of the other walls but seemed fresher.

Eguchi picked up the key. Having done so, he should have gone into the next room; but he remained seated. It was as the woman had said: the sound of the waves was violent. It was as if they were beating against a high cliff, and as if this little house were at its very edge. The wind carried the sound of approaching winter, perhaps because of the house itself, perhaps because of something in old Eguchi. Yet it was quite warm enough with only the single brazier. The district was a warm one. The wind did not seem to be driving leaves before it. Having arrived late, Eguchi had not seen what sort of country the house lay in; but there had been the smell of the sea. The garden was large for the size of the house, with a considerable number of large pines and maples. The needles of the pines lay strong against the sky. The house had probably been a country villa.

The key still in his hand, Eguchi lighted a cigarette. He took a puff or two and put it out; but a second one he smoked to the end. It was less that he was ridiculing himself for the faint apprehension than that he was aware of an unpleasant emptiness. He usually had a little whisky before going to bed. He was a light sleeper, given to bad dreams. A poetess who had died young of cancer had said in one of her poems that for her, on sleepless nights, "the night offers toads and black dogs and corpses of the drowned." It was a line Eguchi could not forget. Remembering it now, he wondered whether the girl asleep— no, put to sleep—in the next room might be like a corpse from a drowning; and he felt some hesitation about going in to her. He had not heard how the girl had been put to sleep. She would in any case be in an unnatural stupor, not conscious of events around her, and so she might have the muddy, leaden skin of one racked by drugs. There might be dark circles under her eyes, her ribs might show through a dry, shriveled skin. Or she might be cold, bloated, puffy. She might be snoring lightly, her lips parted to show purplish gums. In his sixty-seven years, old Eguchi had passed ugly nights with women. Indeed the ugly nights were the hardest ones to forget. The ugliness had had to do not with the appearance of the women but with their tragedies, their warped lives. He did not want to add another such episode, at his age, to the record. So ran his thoughts, on the edge of the adventure. But could there be anything uglier than an old man lying the night through beside a girl put to sleep, unwaking? Had he not come to this house seeking the ultimate in the ugliness of old age?

The woman had spoken of guests she could trust. It seemed that everyone who came here could be trusted. The man who had told Eguchi of the house was so old that he was no longer a man. He seemed to think that Eguchi had reached the same stage of senility. Probably because the woman of the house was accustomed only to making arrangements for such old men, she had turned upon Eguchi a look neither of pity nor of inquiry. Still able to enjoy himself, he was not yet a guest to be trusted; but it was possible to make himself one, because of his feelings at that moment, because of the place, because of his companion. The ugliness of old age pressed down upon him. For him too, he thought, the dreary circumstances of the other guests were not far off. The fact that he was here surely indicated as much. And so he had no intention of breaking the ugly restrictions, the sad restrictions imposed upon the old men. He did not intend to break them, and he would not. Though it might be called a secret club, the number of old men who were members seemed to be few. Eguchi had come neither to expose its sins nor to pry into its secret practices. His curiosity was less than strong, because the dreariness of old age lay already upon him too.

"Some gentlemen say they have good dreams when they come here," the woman had said. "Some say they remember how it was when they were young."

Not even then did a wry smile come over his face. He put his hands to the table and stood up. He went to the cedar door.

"Ah!"

It was the crimson velvet curtains. The crimson was yet deeper in the dim light. It was as if a thin layer of light hovered before the curtains, as if he were stepping into a phantasm. There were curtains over the four walls. The door was curtained too, but the edge had been tied back. He locked the door, drew the curtain, and looked down at the girl. She was not pretending. Her breathing was of the deepest sleep. He caught his breath. She was more beautiful than he had expected. And her beauty was not the only surprise. She was young too. She lay on her left side, her face toward him. He could not see her body—but she would not yet be twenty. It was as if another heart beat its wings in old Eguchi's chest.

Her right hand and wrist were at the edge of the quilt. Her left arm seemed to stretch diagonally under the quilt. Her right thumb was half hidden under her cheek. The fingers on the pillow beside her face were slightly curved in the softness of sleep, though not enough to erase the delicate hollows where they joined the hand. The warm redness was gradually richer from the palm to the fingertips. It was a smooth, glowing white hand.

"Are you asleep? Are you going to wake up?" It was as if he were asking so that he might touch her hand. He took it in his, and shook it. He knew that she would not open her eyes. Her hand still in his, he looked into her face. What kind of girl might she be? The eyebrows were untouched by cosmetics, the closed eyelashes were even. He caught the scent of maidenly hair. After a time the sound of the waves was higher, for his heart had been taken captive. Resolutely he undressed. Noting that the light was from above, he looked up. Electric light came through Japanese paper at two skylights. As if with more composure than was his to muster, he asked himself whether it was a light that set off to advantage the crimson of the velvet, and whether the light from the velvet set off the girl's skin like a beautiful phantom; but the color was not strong enough to show against her skin. He had become accustomed to the light. It was too bright for him, used to sleeping in the dark, but apparently it could not be turned off. He saw that the quilt was a good one.

He slipped quietly under, afraid that the girl he knew would sleep on might awaken. She seemed to be quite naked. There was no reaction, no hunching of the shoulders or pulling in of the hips, to suggest that she sensed his presence. There should be in a young girl, however soundly she slept, some sort of quick reaction. But this would not be an ordinary sleep, he knew. The thought made him avoid touching her as he stretched out. Her knee was slightly forward, leaving his legs in an awkward position. It took no inspection to tell him that she was not on the defensive, that she did not have her right knee resting on her left. The right knee was pulled back, the leg stretched out. The angle of the shoulders as she lay on her left side and that of the hips seemed at variance, because of the inclination of her torso. She did not appear to be very tall.

The fingers of the hand old Eguchi had shaken gently were also in deep sleep. The hand lay as he had dropped it. As he pulled his pillow back the hand fell away. One elbow on the pillow, he gazed at it. As if it were alive, he muttered to himself. It was of course alive, and he meant only to say how very pretty it was; but once he had uttered them the words took on an ominous ring. Though this girl lost in sleep had not put an end to the hours of her life, had she not lost them, had them sink into bottomless depths? She was not a living doll, for there could be no living doll; but, so as not to shame an old man no longer a man, she had been made into a living toy. No, not a toy: for the old men, she could be life itself. Such life was, perhaps, life to be touched with confidence. To Eguchi's farsighted old eyes the hand from close up was yet smoother and more beautiful. It was smooth to the touch, but he could not see the texture.

It came to the old eyes that in the earlobes was the same warm redness of blood that grew richer toward the tips of the fingers. He could see the ears through the hair. The flush of the earlobes argued the freshness of the girl with a plea that stabbed at him. Eguchi had first wandered into this secret house out of curiosity, but it seemed to him that men more senile than he might come to it with even greater happiness and sorrow. The girl's hair was long, possibly for old men to play with. Lying back on his pillow, Eguchi brushed it aside to expose her ear. The sheen of the hair behind the ear was white. The neck and the shoulder too were young and fresh. They did not yet have the fullness of woman. He looked around the room. Only his own clothes were in the box. There was no sign of the girl's. Perhaps the woman had taken them away, but he started up at the thought that the girl might have come into the room naked. She was to be looked at. He knew that she had been put to sleep for the purpose, and that there was no call for this new surprise; but he covered her shoulder and closed his eyes. The scent of a baby came to him in the girl's scent. It was the milky scent of a nursing baby, and richer than that of the girl. Impossible—that the girl should have had a child, that her breasts should be swollen, that milk should be oozing from the nipples. He gazed afresh at her forehead and cheeks, and at the girlish line from the jaw down over the neck. Although he knew well enough already, he slightly raised the quilt that covered the shoulder. The breast was not one that had given milk. He touched it softly with his finger. It was not wet. The girl was approaching twenty. Even if the expression babyish was not wholly inappropriate, she should no longer have the milky scent of a baby. In fact it was a womanish scent. And yet it was very certain that old Eguchi had this very moment smelled a nursing baby. A passing specter? However much he might ask why it had come to him, he did not know the answer; but probably it had come through the opening left by a sudden emptiness in his heart. He felt a surge of loneliness tinged with sorrow. More than sorrow or loneliness, it was the bleakness of old age, as if frozen to him. And it changed to pity and tenderness for the girl who sent out the smell of young warmth. Possibly only for purposes of turning away a cold sense of guilt, the old man seemed to feel music in the girl's body. It was a music of love. As if he wanted to flee, he looked at the four walls, so covered with velvet that there might have been no exit. The crimson velvet, taking its light from the ceiling, was soft and utterly motionless. It shut in a girl who had been put to sleep, and an old man.

"Wake up. Wake up." Eguchi shook at the girl's shoulder. Then he lifted her head. "Wake up. Wake up."

It was a feeling for the girl, rising inside him, that made him do so. A moment had come in which the old man could not bear the fact that the girl was sleeping, that she did not speak, that she did not know his face and his voice; that she knew nothing of what was happening, that she did not know the man Eguchi who was with her. Not the smallest part of his existence reached her. The girl would not wake up, it was the heaviness of a slumbering head in his hand; and yet he could admit the fact that she seemed to frown slightly as a definite living answer. He held his hand motionless. If she were to awaken upon such a slight motion, then the mystery of the place, which old Kiga, the man who had introduced him to it, had described as "like sleep/ ing with a secret Buddha," would be gone. For the old men who were customers the woman could "trust," sleeping with a beauty who would not awaken was a temptation, an adventure, a joy they could trust. Old Kiga had said to Eguchi that only when he was beside a girl who had been put to sleep could he himself feel alive.

When Kiga had visited Eguchi, he had looked out into the garden. Something red lay on the brown autumn moss.

"What can it be?"

He had gone down to look. The dots were red *aoki* berries. Numbers of them lay on the ground. Kiga picked one up. Toying with it, he told Eguchi of the secret house. He went to the house, he said, when the despair of old age was too much for him.

"It seems like a very long time since I lost hope in every last woman. There's a house where they put women to sleep so they don't wake up."

Was it as if a girl sound asleep, saying nothing, hearing noth/ ing, said everything to and heard everything from an old man who, for a woman, was no longer a man? But this was Eguchi's first experience of such a woman. The girl had no doubt had this experience of old men numbers of times before. Giving everything over to him, aware of nothing, in a sleep as of suspended animation, she breathed gently, her innocent face on its side. Certain old men would perhaps caress every part of her body, others would be racked with sobs. The girl would not know, in either case. Even at this thought Eguchi was able to do nothing. In taking his hand from her neck, he was as cautious as if he were handling a breakable object; but the impulse to arouse her by violence still had not left him.

As he withdrew his hand, her head turned gently and her shoulder with it, so that she was lying face up. He pulled back, wondering if she might open her eyes. Her nose and lips shone with youth, in the light from the ceiling. She brought her left hand to her mouth. She seemed about to take the index finger between her teeth, and he wondered if it might be a way she had when she slept; but she brought it softly to her lips, and no further. The lips parted slightly to show her teeth. She had been breathing through her nose, and now she breathed through her mouth. Her breath seemed to come a little faster. He wondered if she might be in pain, and decided she was not. Because the lips were parted, a faint smile seemed to float on the cheeks. The sound of waves breaking against the high cliff came nearer. The sound of the receding waves suggested large rocks at the base of the cliff. Water caught behind them seemed to follow after. The scent of the girl's breath was stronger from her mouth than it had been from her nose. It was not, however, the smell of milk. He asked himself again why the smell of milk had come to him. It was a smell, perhaps, to make him feel woman in the girl.

Old Eguchi even now had a grandchild that smelled of milk. He could see it here before him. Each of his three daughters was married and had children; and he had not forgotten how it had been when they smelled of milk, and how he had held the daughters themselves as nursing babes. Had the milky smell of these blood relatives come back as if to reprove him? No, it would be the smell of Eguchi's own heart, going out to the girl. Eguchi too turned face up, and, lying so that he nowhere touched the girl, closed his eyes. He would do well to take the sleeping medicine at his pillow. It would not be as strong as the drug the girl had been given. He would be awake earlier than she. Otherwise the secret and the fascination of the place would be gone. He opened the packet. In it were two white pills. If he took one he would fall into a slumber; two, and he would fall into a sleep as of death. That would be just as well, he thought, looking at the pills; and the milk brought an unpleasant memory and a lunatic memory to him.

"Milk. It smells of milk. It smells like a baby." Starting to fold the coat he had taken off, the woman glared at him, her face tense. "Your baby. You took it in your arms when you left home, didn't you? Didn't you? I hate it! I hate it!"

Her hands trembling violently, the woman stood up and threw his coat to the floor. "I hate it. Coming here just after you've had a baby in your arms." Her voice was harsh, but the look in her eyes was worse. She was a geisha with whom he had for some time been familiar. She had known all along that he had a wife and children, but the smell of the nursing child brought violent revulsion and jealousy. Eguchi and the geisha were not again on good terms.

The smell the geisha so disliked had been from his youngest child. Eguchi had had a lover before he was married. Her parents became suspicious, and his occasional meetings with her were turbulent. Once when he withdrew his face he saw that her breast was lightly stained with blood. He was startled, but, as if nothing had happened, he brought his face back and gently licked it away. The girl, in a trance, did not know what had happened. The delirium had passed. Even when he told her she did not seem to be in pain.

So far away beyond the years, why had the two memories come back to him? It did not seem likely that because he had had in him the two memories he had smelled milk in the girl beside him. They were far beyond the years, but he did not think, somehow, that one distinguished near memories from distant memories as they were new or old. He might have a fresher and more immediate memory from his boyhood sixty years ago than from only yesterday. Was that tendency not clearer the older one got? Could not a person's young days make him what he was, lead him through life? It was a triviality, but the girl whose breast had been wet with blood had taught him that a man's lips could draw blood from almost any part of a woman's body; and, although afterwards Eguchi had avoided going to that extreme, the memory, the gift from a woman bringing strength to a man's whole life, was still with him, a full sixty-seven years old.

A still more trivial thing.

"Before I go to sleep I close my eyes and count the men I wouldn't mind being kissed by. I count them up on my fingers. It's very pleasant. But it makes me sad when I can't think of even ten." These remarks had been made to the young Eguchi by the wife of a business executive, a middle-aged woman, a woman of society, and, report had it, an intelligent woman. She was waltzing with him at the time. Taking this sudden confession to mean that he was among those she would not mind being kissed by, Eguchi held her hand less tightly.

"I only count them," she said nonchalantly. "You're young, and I suppose you don't find it sad trying to get to sleep. And if you do you always have your wife. But give it a try once in a while. I find it very good medicine."

Her voice was if anything dry, and Eguchi did not answer. She had said that she only counted them; but one could suspect that she called up their faces and bodies in her mind. To conjure up ten would take a considerable amount of time and imagining. At the thought, the perfume as of a love potion from this woman somewhat past her prime came more strongly to Eguchi. She was free to draw in her mind as she wished the figure of Eguchi among the men she would not mind being kissed by. The matter was no concern of his, and he could neither resist nor complain; and yet it was sullying, the fact that without his knowing it he was being enjoyed in the mind of a middle-aged woman. But he had not forgotten her words. He was not without a suspicion afterwards that the woman might have been playing with him, or that she had invented the story to make fun of him; but later still, only the words remained. The woman was long dead. Old Eguchi no longer had these doubts. And, clever woman, she had died after having imagined herself kissing how many hundreds of men?

As old age approached, Eguchi would, on nights when he had difficulty sleeping, sometimes remember the woman's words, and count up numbers of women on his fingers; but he did not stop at anything so simple as picturing those he would not mind kissing. He would travel back over memories of women with whom he had had affairs. An old love had come back tonight because the sleeping beauty had given him the illusion that he smelled milk. Perhaps the blood on the breast of that girl from long ago had made him sense in the girl tonight an odor that

⚶ 26 ⚶

did not exist. Perhaps it was a melancholy comfort for an old man to be sunk in memories of women who would not come back from the far past, even while he fondled a beauty who would not awaken. Eguchi was filled with a warm repose that had loneliness in it. He had but touched her lightly to see whether her breast was wet, and the twisted thought had not come to him of leaving her to be startled, when she awoke after him, at having had blood drawn from her breast. Her breasts seemed to be beautifully rounded. A strange thought came to him: why, among all animals, in the long course of the world, had the breasts of the human female alone become beautiful? Was it not to the glory of the human race to have made woman's breasts so beautiful?

It might be so too with lips. Old Eguchi thought of women getting ready for bed, of women taking off cosmetics before bed. There had been women with pale lips when they took off their lipstick, and women whose lips had shown the dirtiness of age. In the gentle light from the ceiling and the reflection from the velvet on the four walls, it was not clear whether or not the girl was lightly made up, but she had not gone so far as to have her eyebrows shaved. The lips and the teeth between them had a fresh glow. Since she could scarcely have perfumed her mouth, what came to him was the scent of a young woman's mouth. Eguchi did not like wide, dark nipples. From the glimpse he had had when he raised the quilt, it appeared that hers were still small and pink. She was sleeping face up, and he could kiss her breasts. She was certainly not a girl whose breasts he would have disliked kissing. If it was so with a man his age, thought Eguchi, then the really old men who came to the house must quite lose themselves in the joy, be willing to take any chance, to pay any price. There had probably been greedy ones among them, and their images were not wholly absent from Eguchi's mind. The girl was asleep and knew nothing. Would the face and the form remain untouched and unsullied, as they were before him now? Because she was so beautiful asleep, Eguchi stopped short of the ugly act toward which these thoughts led him. Was the difference between him and the other old men that he still had in him something to function as a man? For the others, the girl would pass the night in bottomless sleep. He had twice tried, though gently, to arouse her. He did not himself know what he had meant to do if by chance the girl had opened her eyes, but he had probably made the try out of affection. No, he supposed it had rather been from his own disquiet and emptiness.

"Maybe I should go to sleep?" he heard himself muttering uselessly, and he added: "It's not forever. Not forever, for her or for me."

He closed his eyes. This strange night was, as all other nights, one from which he would wake up alive in the morning. The girl's elbow, as she lay with her index finger touched to her mouth, got in his way. He took her wrist and brought it to his side. He felt her pulse, holding the wrist between his index and middle fingers. It was gentle and regular. Her quiet breath was somewhat slower than Eguchi's. From time to time the wind passed over the house, but it no longer carried the sound of approaching winter. The roar of the waves against the cliff softened while rising. Its echo seemed to come up from the ocean as music sounding in the girl's body, the beating in her breast, and the pulse at her wrist added to it. In time with the music, a pure white butterfly danced past his closed eyelids. He took his hand from her wrist. Nowhere was he touching her. The scent of her breath, of her body, of her hair, were none of them strong.

Eguchi thought of the several days when he had run off to Kyoto, taking the back-country route, with the girl whose breast had been wet with blood. Perhaps the memory was vivid because the warmth of the fresh young body beside him came over to him faintly. There were numerous short tunnels on the railroad from the western provinces into Kyoto. Each time they went into a tunnel, the girl, as if frightened, would bring her knee to Eguchi's and take his hand. And each time they came out of one there would be a hill or a small ravine with a rainbow over it.

"How pretty," she would say each time, or "How nice." She had a word of praise for each little rainbow, and it would be no exaggeration to say that, searching to the left and the right, she found one each time they came out of a tunnel. Sometimes it would be so faint as to be hardly there at all. She came to feel something ominous in these strangely abundant rainbows.

"Don't you suppose they're after us? I have a feeling they'll catch us when we get to Kyoto. Once they take me back they won't let me out of the house again."

Eguchi, who had just graduated from college and gone to work, had no way to make a living in Kyoto, and he knew that, unless he and the girl committed suicide together, they would presently have to go back to Tokyo; but, from the small rainbows, the cleanness of the girl's secret parts came before him and would not leave. He had seen it at an inn by a river in Kanazawa. It had been on a night of snow flurries. So struck had he been by the cleanness that he had held his breath and felt tears welling up. He had not seen such cleanness in the women of all the decades since; and he had come to think that he understood all cleanness, that cleanness in secret places was the girl's own property. He tried to laugh the notion away, but it became a fact in the flow of longing, and it was still a powerful memory, not to be shaken from the old Eguchi. A person sent by the girl's family took her back to Tokyo, and soon she was married.

When they chanced to meet by Shinobazu Pond, the girl had a baby strapped to her back. The baby had on a white wool cap. It was autumn and the lotuses in the pond were withering. Possibly the white butterfly dancing behind his closed eyelids tonight was called up by that white cap.

When they met by the pond, all Eguchi could think of was to ask whether she was happy.

"Yes," she replied immediately. "I am happy." Probably there was no other answer.

"And why are you walking here all by yourself with a baby on your back?" It was a strange question. The girl only looked into his face.

"Is it a boy or a girl?"

"It's a girl. Really! Can't you tell by looking at it?"

"Is it mine?"

"It is not." The girl shook her head angrily. "It is not."

"Oh? Well, if it is, you needn't say so now. You can say so when you feel like it. Years and years from now."

"It is not. It really is not. I haven't forgotten that I loved you, but you are not to imagine things. You will only cause trouble for her."

"Oh?" Eguchi made no special attempt to look at the baby's face, but he looked on and on after the girl. She glanced back when she had gone some distance. Seeing that he was still watching her, she quickened her pace. He did not see her again. More than ten years ago he had heard of her death. Eguchi, now sixty-seven, had lost many friends and relations, but the memory of the girl was still young. Reduced now to three details, the baby's white cap and the cleanness of the secret place and the blood on the breast, it was still clear and fresh. Probably there was no one in the world besides Eguchi who knew of that incomparable cleanness, and with his death, not far away now, it would quite disappear from the world. Though shyly, she had let him look on as he would. Perhaps that was the way with girls; but there could be no doubt that the girl did not herself know of the cleanness. She could not see it.

Early in the morning after they got to Kyoto, Eguchi and the girl walked through a bamboo grove. The bamboo shimmered silver in the morning light. In Eguchi's memory the leaves were fine and soft, of pure silver, and the bamboo stalks were of silver too. On the path that skirted the grove, thistles and dew-flowers were in bloom. Such was the path that floated up in his memory. There would seem to be some confusion about the season. Beyond the path they climbed a blue stream, where a waterfall roared down, its spray catching the sunlight. In the spray the girl stood naked. The facts were different, but in the course of time Eguchi's mind had made them so. As he grew old, the hills of Kyoto and the trunks of the red pines in gentle clusters could sometimes bring the girl back to Eguchi; but memories as vivid as tonight's were rare. Was it the youth of the sleeping girl that invited them?

Old Eguchi was wide awake and did not seem likely to go to sleep. He did not want to remember women other than the girl who had looked at the little rainbows. Nor did he want to touch the sleeping girl, to look at her naked. Turning face down, he again opened the packet at his pillow. The woman of the inn had said that it was sleeping medicine, but Eguchi hesitated. He did not know what it would be, whether or not it would be the medicine the girl had been given. He took one pill in his mouth, and washed it down with a good amount of water. Perhaps because he was used to a bedtime drink but not to sleeping medicine, he was quickly pulled into sleep. He had a dream.

He was in the embrace of a woman, but she had four legs. The four legs were entwined about him. She had arms as well. Though half awake, he thought the four legs odd, but not repulsive. Those four legs, so much more provocative than two, were still with him. It was a medicine to make one have such dreams, he thought absently. The girl had turned away from him, her hips toward him. He seemed to find something touching about the fact that her head was more distant than her hips. Half asleep and half awake, he took the long hair spread out toward him and played with it as if to comb it; and so he fell asleep.

His next dream was most unpleasant. One of his daughters had borne a deformed child in a hospital. Awake, the old man could not remember what sort of deformity it had been. Probably he did not want to remember. It was hideous, in any case. The baby was immediately taken from the mother. It was behind a white curtain in the maternity room, and she went over and commenced hacking it to pieces, getting it ready to throw away. The doctor, a friend of Eguchi's, was standing beside her in white. Eguchi too was beside her. He was wide awake now, groaning from the horror of it. The crimson velvet on the four walls so startled him that he put his hands to his face and rubbed his forehead. It had been a horrible nightmare. There could scarcely be a monster hidden in the sleeping medicine. Was it that, having come in search of misshapen pleasure, he had had a misshapen dream? He did not know which of his three daughters he had dreamed of, and he did not try to know. All three had borne quite normal babies.

Eguchi would have wanted to leave if it had been possible. But he took the other pill, to fall into a deeper sleep. The cold water passed down his throat. The girl still had her back to him. Thinking that she might—it was not impossible—bear the ugliest and most doltish of children, he put his hand to the roundness at her shoulder.

"Look this way."

As if in answer she turned over. One of her hands fell on his chest. One leg came toward him, as if trembling in the cold. So warm a girl could not be cold. From her mouth or her nose, he could not be sure which, came a small voice.

"Are you having a nightmare too?" he asked.

But old Eguchi was quick to sink into the depths of sleep.

2

Old Eguchi had not thought that he would again go the "house of the sleeping beauties." He had not thought when he spent that first night there that he would like to go again. So it had been too when he left in the morning.

It was about a fortnight later that a telephone call came asking whether he might like to pay a visit that night. The voice seemed to be that of the woman in her forties. Over the telephone it sounded even more like a cold whisper from a silent place.

"If you leave now, when may I hope to see you?"

"A little after nine, I'd imagine."

"That will be too soon. The young lady is not here yet, and even if she were she would not be asleep."

Startled, Eguchi did not answer.

"I should have her asleep by eleven. I'll be waiting for you any time after that."

The woman's speech was slow and calm, but Eguchi's heart raced.

"About eleven, then," he said, his throat dry.

What does it matter whether she's asleep or not, he should have been able to say, not seriously, perhaps, but half in jest. He would have liked to meet her before she went to sleep, he could have said. But somehow the words caught in his throat. He had come up against the secret rule of the house. Because it was such a strange rule, it had to be followed all the more strictly. Once it was broken, the place became no more than an ordinary bawdy house. The sad requests of the old men, the allurements, all disappeared. Eguchi himself was startled at the fact that he had caught his breath so sharply upon being told that nine was too early, that the girl would not be asleep, that the woman would have her asleep by eleven. Might it be called the surprise of suddenly being pulled away from the everyday world? For the girl would be asleep and certain not to wake up.

Was he too quick or too slow, going again after a fortnight to a house he had not thought to revisit? He had not, in any case, resisted the temptation by force of will. He had not meant to indulge again in this sort of ugly senile dalliance, and in fact he was not yet as senile as the other men who visited the place. And yet that first visit had not left behind ugly memories. The guilt was there; but he felt that he had not in all his sixty-seven years spent another night so clean. So he still felt when he awoke in the morning. The sleeping medicine had worked, it seemed, and he had slept until eight, later than usual. No part of him was touching the girl. It was a sweet, childlike awakening, in her young warmth and soft scent.

The girl had lain with her face toward him, her head very slightly forward and her breasts back, and in the shadow of her jaw there had been a scarcely perceptible line across the fresh, slender neck. Her long hair was spread over the pillow behind her. Looking up from the neatly closed lips, he had gazed at her eyebrows and eyelashes, and had not doubted that she was a virgin. She was too near for his old eyes to make out the individual hairs of the eyelashes and eyebrows. Her skin, on which he could not see the fuzz, glowed softly. There was not a single mole on the face and neck. He had forgotten the nightmare, and as affection for the girl poured through him, there came over him too a childlike feeling that he was loved by the girl. He felt for a breast, and held it softly in his hand. There was in the touch a strange flicker of something, as if this were the breast of Eguchi's own mother before she had him inside her. He withdrew his hand, but the sensation went from his chest to his shoulders.

He heard the door to the next room open.

"Are you awake?" asked the woman of the house. "I have breakfast ready."

"Yes," said Eguchi hastily. The morning sun through the shutters fell bright on the velvet curtains. But morning light did not mix with the soft light from the ceiling.

"I can bring it, then?"

"Yes."

Raising himself, Eguchi softly touched the girl's hair.

He knew that the woman was sending her customer away before the girl awoke, but she was calm as she served him breakfast. Until when had the girl been put to sleep? But it would not do to ask unnecessary questions.

"A very pretty girl," he said nonchalantly.

"Yes. And did you have pleasant dreams?"

"It brought me very pleasant dreams."

"The wind and the waves have quieted down." The woman changed the subject. "It will be what they call Indian summer."

And now, coming a second time in half a month, Eguchi did

not feel the curiosity of the earlier visit so much as reticence and a certain discomfort; but the excitement was also stronger. The impatience of the wait from nine to eleven had brought on a certain intoxication.

The same woman unlocked the gate for him. The same reproduction was in the alcove. The tea was again good. He was more nervous than on his earlier visit, but he managed to behave like an old and experienced customer.

"It's so warm hereabouts," he said, looking around at the picture of the mountain village in autumn leaves, "that I imagine the maple leaves wither without really turning red. But then it was dark, and I didn't really get a good look at your garden."

It was an improbable way to make conversation.

"I wonder," said the woman, indifferently. "It's gotten very cold. I've put on an electric blanket, a double one with two switches. You can adjust your side to suit yourself."

"I've never slept under an electric blanket."

"You can turn your side off if you like, but I must ask that you leave the girl's on."

Because she was naked, the old man knew.

"An interesting idea, a blanket that two people can adjust to suit themselves."

"It's American. But please don't be difficult and turn off the girl's side. You understand, I'm sure, that she won't wake up, no matter how cold she gets."

He did not answer.

"She's more experienced than the one before."

"What?"

"She's very pretty too. You won't do anything wrong, I know —and so it wouldn't be right if she weren't pretty."

"It's not the same one?"

"No. This evening—isn't it better to have a different one?"

"I'm not as promiscuous as all that."

"Promiscuous? But what does it have to do with promiscuousness?"

The woman's easy way of speaking seemed to hide a faint smile of derision. "None of my guests do anything promiscuous. They are all kind enough to be gentlemen I can trust." Thin-lipped, the woman did not look at him as she spoke. The note of mockery set Eguchi on edge, but he could think of nothing to say. What was she, after all, but a cold, seasoned procuress?

"And then you may think of it as promiscuous, but the girl herself is asleep, and doesn't even know who she has slept with. The girl the other time and the girl tonight will never know a thing about you, and to speak of promiscuousness is a little . . ."

"I see. It's not a human relationship."

"What do you mean?"

It would be odd to explain, now that he had come to the house, that for an old man who was no longer a man, to keep company with a girl who had been put to sleep was "not a human relationship."

"And what's wrong with being promiscuous?" Her voice strangely young, the woman laughed a laugh to soothe an old man. "If you're so fond of the other girl, I can have her here the next time you come; but you'll admit afterwards that this one is better."

"Oh? What do you mean when you say she's more experienced? After all she's sound asleep."

"Yes." The woman got up, unlocked the door to the next room, looked inside, and put the key before old Eguchi. "I hope you sleep well."

Eguchi poured hot water into the pot and had a leisurely cup of tea. He meant it to be leisurely, at least, but his hand was shaking. It was not because of his age, he muttered. He was not yet a guest to be trusted. How would it be, by way of revenge for all the derided and insulted old men who came here, if he were to violate the rule of the house? And would that not be a more human way of keeping company with the girl? He did not know how heavily she had been drugged, but he was probably still capable of awakening her with his roughness. So he thought; but his heart did not rise to the challenge.

The ugly senility of the sad men who came to this house was not many years away for Eguchi himself. The immeasurable expanse of sex, its bottomless depth—what part of it had Eguchi known in his sixty-seven years? And around the old men, new flesh, young flesh, beautiful flesh was forever being born. Were not the longing of the sad old men for the unfinished dream, the regret for days lost without ever being had, concealed in the secret of this house? Eguchi had thought before that girls who did not awaken were ageless freedom for old men. Asleep and un-speaking, they spoke as the old men wished.

He got up and opened the door to the next room, and already a warm smell came to him. He smiled. Why had he hesitated? The girl lay with both hands on the quilt. Her nails were pink. Her lipstick was a deep red. She lay face up.

"Experienced, is she?" he muttered as he came up to her. Her cheeks were flushed from the warmth of the blanket, and indeed her whole face was flushed. The scent was rich. Her eyelids and cheeks were full. Her neck was so white as to take on the crimson of the velvet curtains. The closed eyes seemed to tell him that a young witch lay sleeping before him. As he undressed, his back to her, the warm smell enveloped him. The room was filled with it.

It did not seem likely that old Eguchi could be as reticent as he had been with the other girl. This was a girl who, whether sleeping or awake, called out to a man—so strongly that, were he to violate the rule of the house, he could only blame the misdeed on her. He lay with his eyes closed, as if to savor the pleasure that was to come later, and youthful warmth came up from deep inside him. The woman had spoken well when she said that this one was better; but the house seemed all the stranger for having been able to find such a girl. He lay wrapped in the perfume, thinking her too good to touch. Though he did not know a great deal about perfume, this seemed to be the scent of the girl herself. There could be no greater happiness than thus drifting off into a sweet sleep. He wanted to do just that. He slid quietly toward her. As though in reply, she turned gently toward him, her arms extended under the blanket as if to embrace him.

"Are you awake?" he asked, pulling away and shaking her jaw. "Are you awake?" He put more strength into his hand. She turned face down as if to avoid it, and as she did so a corner of her mouth opened slightly, and the nail of his index finger brushed against one or two of her teeth. He left it there. Her lips remained parted. She was of course in a deep sleep, and not merely pretending.

Not expecting the girl tonight to be different from the girl of the other night, he had protested to the woman of the house; but he knew of course that to take sleeping medicine repeatedly could only injure a girl. It might be said that for the sake of the girls' health Eguchi and the other old men were made to be "promiscuous." But were not these upstairs rooms for a single guest only? Eguchi did not know much about the first floor, but if it was for guests at all it could not have more than one guest room. He hardly thought, then, that many girls were needed for the old men who came here. And were they all beautiful in their different ways, like the girl tonight and the one before?

The tooth against Eguchi's finger seemed to be very slightly damp with something that clung to the finger. He moved it back and forth in her mouth, feeling the teeth two and three times. On the outside they were for the most part dry, but on the inside they were smooth and damp. To the right they were crooked, a tooth on top of another. He took the crooked pair between his thumb and index finger. He thought of putting his finger behind them, but, though asleep, she clenched her teeth and quite refused to open them. When he took his finger away it was stained red. And with what was he to wipe away the lip-stick? If he wiped it on the pillow case, it would look as if she had smeared it herself when she turned face down. But it did not seem likely to come off unless he moistened it with his tongue, and he was strangely revolted at the thought of touching his mouth to the red finger. He rubbed it against the hair at her forehead. Rubbing with his thumb and index finger, he was soon probing through her hair with all five fingers, twisting it; and gradually his motions were rougher. The ends of the girl's hair sent out little sparks of electricity against his fingers. The scent from the hair was stronger. Partly because of the warmth of the electric blanket, the scent from under it too was stronger. As he played with her hair, he noted the lines at the edges, clean as if sketched in, and especially the line at the nape of the long neck, where the hair was short and brushed upwards. At the forehead long hair and short hair fell in strands, as if untended. Brushing it upwards he gazed at her eyebrows and eyelashes. The other hand was so deep in her hair that he could feel the skin beneath.

"No, she's not awake," he said to himself, clutching at her hair and shaking from the crown.

She seemed in pain, and rolled over face down. The motion brought her nearer the old man. Both arms were exposed. The right arm was on the pillow. The right cheek rested on it, so that Eguchi could see only the fingers. They were slightly spread, the little finger below the eyelashes, the index finger at her lips. The thumb was hidden under her chin. The red of her lips, inclined somewhat downwards, and the red of the four long fingernails made a cluster along the white pillowcase. The left arm too was bent at the elbow. The hand was almost directly under Eguchi's eyes. The fingers, long and slender compared to the fullness of the cheeks, made him think of her outstretched legs. He felt for a leg with the sole of his foot. The left hand too lay with the fingers slightly parted. He rested his head on it. A spasm caused by his weight went all the way to her shoulder, but it was not enough to pull the hand away. He lay unmoving for a time. Her shoulders were slightly raised, and there was a young roundness in them. As he pulled the blanket over them, he took the roundness gently in his hand. He moved his face from her hand to her arm. He was drawn by the scent of the shoulder, the nape of the neck. There was a tremor along the shoulder and the back, but it passed immediately. The old man clung to them.

He would now have revenge upon this slave maiden, drugged into sleep, for all the contempt and derision endured by the old men who frequented the house. He would violate the rule of the house. He knew that he would not be allowed to come again. He hoped to awaken her by his roughness. But immediately he drew back, for he had come upon clear evidence of her virginity.

He groaned as he pulled away, his breathing was convulsive, his pulse rapid, less from the sudden interruption than from the surprise. He closed his eyes and tried to calm himself. It was easy for him as it would not have been for a young man. Stroking her hair, he opened his eyes again. She still lay face downward. A virgin prostitute, and at her age! What was she if not a prostitute? So he told himself; but with the passage of the storm his feelings toward the girl and his feelings toward himself had changed, and would not return to what they had been. He was not sorry. It would have been the merest folly, whatever he might have done to a sleeping and unknowing girl. But what had been the meaning of the surprise?

Led astray by the witchlike face, Eguchi had set out upon the forbidden path; and now he knew that the old men who were guests here came with a happiness more melancholy, a craving far stronger, a sadness far deeper that he had imagined. Though theirs was an easy sort of dalliance for old men, an easy way to juvenescence, it had deep inside it something that would not come back whatever the regrets, that would not be healed however strenuous the efforts. That the "experienced" witch tonight was still a virgin was less the mark of the old men's respect for their promises than the grim mark of their decline. The purity of the girl was like the ugliness of the old men.

Perhaps the hand beneath her cheek had gone numb. She brought it over her head and slowly flexed the fingers two or three times. It touched Eguchi's hand, still probing through her hair. He took it in his. The fingers where supple and a little cold. He ground them together, as if to crush them. Raising her left shoulder, she turned half over. She brought her left arm up and flung it over Eguchi's shoulder as if to embrace him. It was without strength, however, and did not take his neck in its embrace. Her face, now turned toward him, was too near, a blurry white to his old eyes; but the too-thick eyebrows, the eyelashes casting too dark a shadow, the full eyelids and cheeks, the long neck, all confirmed his first impression, that of a witch.

The breasts sagged slightly but were very full, and for a Japanese the nipples were large and swollen. He ran a hand down her spine and over her legs. They were stretched taut from the hips. What seemed like a disharmony between the upper and lower parts of her body may have had to do with her being a virgin.

Quietly now, he looked at her face and neck. It was a skin meant to take on a faint reflection from the crimson of the velvet curtains. Her body had so been used by old men that the woman of the house had described her as "experienced," and yet she was a virgin. It was because the men were senile, and because she was in such a deep sleep. Thoughts almost fatherly came to him as he asked himself what vicissitudes this witchlike girl faced through the years ahead. In them was evidence that Eguchi too was old. There could be no doubt that the girl was here for money. Nor was there any doubt that, for the old men who paid out the money, sleeping beside such a girl was a happiness not of this world. Because the girl would not awaken, the aged guests need not feel the shame of their years. They were quite free to indulge in unlimited dreams and memories of women. Was that not why they felt no hesitation at paying more than for women awake? And the old men were confident in the knowledge that the girls put to sleep for them knew nothing of them. Nor did the old men know anything of the girls—not even what clothes they wore—to give clues of position and character. The reasons went beyond such simple matters as disquiet about later complications. They were a strange light at the bottom of a deep darkness.

But old Eguchi was not yet used to keeping company with a girl who said nothing, a girl who did not open her eyes, who gave him no recognition. Empty longing had not left him. He wanted to see the eyes of this witchlike girl. He wanted to hear her voice, to talk to her. The urge was not so strong to explore the sleeping girl with his hands. Indeed it had in it a certain bleak-ness. Having been startled into rejecting all thoughts of violating the secret rule, he would follow the ways of the other old men. The girl tonight, though asleep, was more alive than the girl the other night. Life was there, most definitely, in her scent, in her touch, in the way she moved.

As before, two sleeping pills lay beside his pillow. But tonight he thought he would not go to sleep immediately. He would look yet a time longer at the girl. Her movements were strong, even in her sleep. It seemed that she must turn over twenty or thirty times in the course of a night. She turned away from him, and immediately turned back again. She felt for him with her arm. He reached for a knee and brought it toward him.

"Don't," the girl seemed to say, in a voice that was not a voice.

"Are you awake?" He pulled more strongly at the knee, to see whether she would awaken. Weakly, it bent toward him. He put his arm under her neck and gently shook her head.

"Ah," said the girl. "Where am I going?"

"Are you awake? Wake up."

"Don't, don't." Her face brushed against his shoulder, as if to avoid the shaking. Her forehead touched his neck, her hair was against his nose. It was stiff, even painful. Eguchi turned away from the too-strong odor.

"What do you think you're doing?" said the girl. "Stop it."

"I'm not doing a thing."

But she was talking in her sleep. Had she in her sleep mis-understood his motions, or was she dreaming of having been mistreated by some other old man on some other night? His heart beat faster at the thought that, even though what she said was in bits and fragments, he could have something like a conversation with her. Perhaps in the morning he could awaken her. But had she really heard him? Was it not less his words than his touch that made her talk in her sleep? He thought of striking her a smart blow, of pinching her; but instead he brought her slowly into his arms. She did not resist, nor did she speak. She seemed to find it hard to breathe. Her breath came sweetly against the old man's face. His own breathing was irregular. He was aroused again by this girl who was his to do with as he wished. What sort of sadness would assail her in the morning if he made a woman of her? How would the direction of her life be changed? She would in any case know nothing until morning.

"Mother." It was like a low groan. "Wait, wait. Do you have to go? I'm sorry, I'm sorry."

"What are you dreaming of? It's a dream, a dream." Old Eguchi took her more tightly in his arms, thinking to end the dream. The sadness in her voice stabbed at him. Her breasts were pressed flat against him. Her arms moved. Was she trying to embrace him, thinking him her mother? No, even though she had been put to sleep, even though she was a virgin, the girl was unmistakably a witch. It seemed to Eguchi that he had not in all his sixty-seven years felt so fully the skin of a young witch. If somewhere there was a weird legend demanding a heroine, this was the girl for it.

It came to seem that she was not the witch but the bewitched. And she was alive while asleep. Her mind had been put into a deep sleep and her body had awakened as a woman. She had become a woman's body, without mind. And was it so well trained that the woman of the house called it "experienced."

He relaxed his embrace and put her bare arms around him as if to make her embrace him; and she did, gently. He lay still, his eyes closed. He was warmly drowsy, in a sort of mindless rapture. He seemed to have awakened to the feelings of well-being, of good fortune, that came to the old men who frequented the house. Did the sadness, ugliness, dreariness of old age leave the old men, were they filled with the blessings of young life? There could be for an old man worn to the point of death no time of greater oblivion than when he lay enveloped in the skin of a young girl. But was it without feelings of guilt that the old men paid money for young girls who were sacrificed to them; or did secret feelings of guilt actually add to the pleasure? As if, forgetting himself, he had forgotten that the girl was a sacrifice, he felt for her toes with his foot. It was only her toes that he had not already touched. They were long and supple. As with her fingers, every joint bent and unbent freely, and in that small detail the lure of the strange in the girl came over to Eguchi. The girl spoke words of love with her toes as she lay sleeping. But the old man stopped at hearing in them a childish and uncertain and yet voluptuous music; and for a time he listened.

She had been dreaming. Was the dream over now? Perhaps it had not been a dream. Perhaps the heavy touch of old men had trained her to talk in her sleep, to resist. Was that it? She overflowed with a sensuousness that made it possible for her body to converse in silence; but probably because he was not entirely used to the secret of the house, the wish to hear her voice even as she spoke little fragments in her sleep was still with Eguchi. He wondered what he should say, where he should touch, to get an answer from her.

"You aren't dreaming any more? Dreaming that your mother went away?"

He probed into the hollows along her spine. She shook her shoulders and again turned face down—it seemed to be a position she liked. She turned toward Eguchi again. With her right hand she gently held the edge of the pillow, and her left arm rested on Eguchi's face. But she said nothing. Her soft breath came warmly to him. She moved the arm on his face, evidently seeking a more comfortable position. He took it in both hands and put it over his eyes. Her long fingernails cut gently into the lobe of his ear. Her wrist bent over his right eye, its narrowest part pressing down on the eyelid. Wanting to keep it there, he held it in place with his hands. The scent that came through to his eyes was new to him again, and it brought rich new fantasies. Just at this time of year, two or three winter peonies blooming in the warm sun, under the high stone fence of an old temple in Yamato. White camellias in the garden near the veranda of the Shisendō.[1] In the spring, wistaria and white rhododendrons in Nara; the "petal-dropping" camellia, filling the garden of the Camellia Temple in Kyoto.

That was it. The flowers brought memories of his three married daughters. They were flowers he had seen on trips with the three, or with one of them. Now wives and mothers, they probably did did not have such vivid memories themselves. Eguchi remembered well, and sometimes spoke of the flowers to his wife. She apparently did not feel as far from the daughters, now that they were married, as did Eguchi. She was still close to them, and need not dwell so on memories of flowers seen with them. And there were flowers from trips when she had not been along.

Far back in the eyes on which the girl's hand rested, he let the images of flowers come up and fade away, fade away and come up; and feelings returned of the days when, his daughters married, he had been drawn to other young girls. It seemed to him that

---

1. The residence in Kyoto of Ishikawa Jōzan (1583–1672), a scholar and calligrapher.

the girl tonight was one of them. He released her arm, but it lay quiet over his eyes. Only his youngest daughter had been with him when he had seen the great camellia. It had been on a farewell trip he had taken with her a fortnight before she was married. The image of the camellia was especially strong. The marriage of his youngest daughter had been the most painful. Two youths had been in competition for her, and in the course of the competition she had lost her virginity. The trip had been a change of scenery, to revive her spirits.

Camellias are said to be bad luck because the flowers drop whole from the stem, like severed heads; but the double blossoms on this great tree, which was four hundred years old and bloomed in five different colors, fell petal by petal. Hence it was called the "petal-dropping" camellia.

"When they are thickest," said the young wife of the priest to Eguchi, "we gather up five or six baskets a day."

The massing of flowers on the great camellia was less beautiful in the full sunlight, he was told, than with the sunlight behind it. Eguchi and his youngest daughter were sitting on the western veranda, and the sun was sinking behind the tree. They were looking into the sun; but the thick leaves and the clusters of flowers did not let the sunlight through. It sank into the camellia, as if the evening sun itself were hanging on the edges of the shadow. The Camellia Temple was in a noisy, vulgar part of the city, and there was nothing to see in the garden besides the camellia. Eguchi's eyes were filled with it, and he did not hear the noise of the city.

"It *is* in fine bloom," he said to his daughter.

"Sometimes when you get up in the morning there are so many petals that you can't see the ground," said the young wife, leaving Eguchi and his daughter.

Were there five colors on the one tree? He could see red camellias and white, and camellias with crinkled petals. But Eguchi was not particularly interested in verifying the number of colors. He was quite caught up in the tree itself. It was remark- able that a tree four hundred years old could produce such a richness of blossoms. The whole of the evening light was sucked into the camellia, so that the inside of the tree must be warm with it. Although he could feel no wind, a branch at the edge would rustle from time to time.

It did not seem that his youngest daughter was as lost in the famous tree as Eguchi himself. There was no strength in her eyes. Perhaps she was less gazing at the tree than looking into herself. She was his favorite among his daughters, and she had the willfulness of a youngest child, even more so now that her sisters were married. The older girls had asked their mother, with some jealousy, if Eguchi did not mean to keep the youngest at home and bring a bridegroom into the family for her. His wife had passed the remark on to him. His youngest daughter had grown up a bright and lively girl. It seemed to him unwise for her to have so many men friends, and then again she was liveliest when she was surrounded by men. But that there were among them all two whom she liked was clear to her parents, and especially to her mother, who saw a good deal of them. One of them had taken her virginity. For a time she was silent and moody even in the security of the house, and she seemed impatient and irritable when, for instance, she was changing clothes. Her mother sensed that something had happened. She asked about it in a casual fashion, and the girl showed little hesitation in making her confession. The young man worked in a depart- ment store and had a rented room. The girl seemed to have gone meekly home with him.

"Is he the one you mean to marry?"

"No. Absolutely no," replied the girl, leaving her mother in some confusion.

The mother was sure that the youth had had his way by force. She talked the matter over with Eguchi. For Eguchi it was as though the jewel in his hand had been scarred. He was still more shocked when he learned that the girl had rushed into betrothal with the other suitor.

"What do you think?" asked Eguchi's wife, leaning tensely toward him. "Is it all right?"

"Has she told the man she's engaged to?" Eguchi's voice was sharp. "Has she?"

"I wonder. I didn't ask. I was too surprised myself. Shall I ask?"

"Don't bother."

"Most people seem to think it's best not to tell the man you're going to marry. It's safest to be quiet. But we aren't all alike. She may suffer her whole life through if she doesn't tell him."

"But we haven't decided that she has our permission."

It did not, of course, seem natural to Eguchi that a girl accosted by one young man should suddenly become engaged to another. He knew that both were fond of his daughter. Well acquainted with both, he had thought that either would do for her. But was not this sudden engagement a rebound from the shock? Had she not turned to the second young man in bitterness, resentment, chagrin? Was she not, in the turmoil of her disillusionment with the one, throwing herself at the other? A girl like his youngest daughter might very well turn the more ardently to one young man from having been molested by another. They need not, perhaps, reprove her for an unworthy act of revenge and self-abasement.

But it had not occurred to Eguchi that such a thing could happen to his daughter. So probably it was with all parents. Eguchi may have had too much confidence in his high-spirited daughter, so open and lively when surrounded by men. But now that the deed was done there seemed nothing strange about it. Her body was put together in a manner no different from the bodies of other women. A man could force himself upon her. At the thought of her unsightliness in the act, Eguchi was assailed by strong feelings of shame and degradation. No such feelings had come to him when he had sent his older daughters on their honeymoons. What had happened may have been an explosion of love on the part of the youth; but it had happened, and Eguchi could only reflect upon how his daughter's body was made, upon its inability to turn the act away. Were such reflections abnormal for a father? Eguchi did not immediately sanction the engagement, nor did he reject it. He and his wife learned considerably later that the competition between the youths had been rather vicious. His daughter's marriage was near when he took her to Kyoto and they saw the camellia in full bloom. There was a faint roar inside it, like a swarm of honeybees.

She had a son two years after she was married. Her husband seemed quite wrapped up in the child. When, perhaps on a Sunday, the young couple would come to Eguchi's house, the wife would go out to help her mother in the kitchen, and the husband, most deftly, would feed the baby. And so matters had resolved themselves nicely. Although she lived in Tokyo, the daughter seldom came to see them after she was married.

"How are you?" Eguchi asked once when she came alone.

"How am I? Happy, I suppose."

Perhaps people did not have a great deal to say to their parents about their marital relations, but Eguchi was somehow dissatisfied and a trifle disturbed. Given the nature of his youngest daughter, it seemed to him that she ought to say more. But she was more beautiful, she had come into bloom. Even though the change might be the physiological one from girl to young wife, it did not seem that there would be this flower-like brightness if a shadow lay over her heart. After she had her baby her skin was clearer, as though she had been washed to the depths, and she seemed more in possession of herself.

And was that it? Was that why, in "the house of the sleeping beauties," as he lay with the girl's arm over his eyes, the images of the camellia in full bloom and the other flowers came to him? There was of course neither in the girl sleeping here nor in Eguchi's youngest daughter the richness of the camellia. But the richness of a girl's body was not something one knew by looking at her or by lying quietly beside her. It was not to be compared with the richness of camellias. What flowed deep behind his eyelids from the girl's arm was the current of life, the melody of life, the lure of life, and, for an old man, the recovery of life. The eyes on which the girl's arm rested were heavy, and he took the arm away.

There was nowhere for her to put her left arm. Probably because it was awkward for her to stretch it taut along Eguchi's chest, she half turned over to face him again. She brought both hands together over her bosom with the fingers interlocked. They touched Eguchi's chest. They were not clasped as in veneration, but still they suggested prayer, soft prayer. He took the two clasped hands between his own hands. It was as if he were praying for something himself. He closed his eyes, probably in nothing more than the sadness of an old man touching the hands of a sleeping young girl.

He heard the first drops of night rain falling on the quiet sea.

The distant sound seemed to come not from an automobile but from the thunder of winter. It was not easy to catch. He unfolded the girl's hands and gazed at the fingers as he straightened them one by one. He wanted to take the long, slender fingers in his mouth. What would she think, awakening the next morning, if there were toothmarks on her little finger and blood oozing from it? Eguchi brought the girl's arm down along her body. He looked at her rich breasts, the nipples large and swollen and dark. He raised them, gently sagging as they were. They were not as warm as her body, warmed by the electric blanket. He thought to bring his forehead to the hollow between them, but only drew near, and held back because of the scent. He rolled over face down and this time took both the sleeping tablets at once. On the earlier visit he had taken one tablet, and then taken the other when he had awakened from a nightmare; but he had learned that they were only sleeping medicine. He was quick to fall asleep.

The voice of the girl sobbing awakened him. Then what sounded like sobs changed to laughter. The laughter went on and on. He put his arm over her breasts and shook her.

"You're dreaming, you're dreaming. What are you dreaming of?"

There was something ominous in the silence that followed the laughter. But Eguchi too was heavy with sleep, and it was all he could do to feel for the watch at his pillow. It was three-thirty. Bringing his chest to her and drawing her hips toward him, he slept a warm sleep.

The next morning he was again aroused by the woman of the house.

"Are you awake?"

He did not answer. Did the woman not have her ear to the

door of the secret room? A spasm went through him at indica-
tions that was indeed the case. Perhaps because of the heat from
the blanket, the girl's shoulders were exposed, and she had an
arm over her head. He pulled the quilt up.

"Are you awake?"

Still not answering, he put his head under the quilt. A breast
touched his chin. It was as if he were suddenly on fire. He put his
arm around the girl's back and pulled her toward him with his
foot.

"Sir! Sir!" The woman rapped on the door three or four
times.

"I'm awake. I'm getting dressed." It seemed that she would
come into the room if he did not answer.

The woman had brought water and toothpaste and the like
into the next room.

"And how was it?" she asked as she served his breakfast.
"Don't you think she's a good girl?"

"A very good girl," Eguchi nodded. "When will she wake
up?"

"I wonder."

"Can't I stay until she's awake?"

"That's exactly the sort of thing we can't allow," the woman
said hastily. "We don't allow that even with our oldest guests."

"But she's *too* good a girl."

"It's best just to keep them company and not let foolish emo-
tions get in the way. She doesn't even know she's slept with you.
She won't cause you any trouble."

"But I remember her. What if we were to pass in the street?"

"You mean you might speak to her? Don't do that. It would
be a crime."

"A crime?"

"It would indeed."

"A crime."

"I must ask you not to be difficult. Just take sleeping girls as sleeping girls." He wanted to retort that he had not yet reached that sad degree of senility, but held himself back.

"I believe there was rain last night," he said.

"Really? I didn't notice."

"I definitely heard rain."

On the sea outside the window little waves caught the morning sunlight in near the cliff.

3

Eight days after his second visit old Eguchi went again to the "house of the sleeping beauties." It had been two weeks between his first and second visits, and so the interval had been cut in half.

Was he gradually being pulled in by the spell of girls put to sleep?

"The one tonight is still in training," said the woman of the house as she made tea. "You may be disappointed, but please put up with her."

"A different one again?"

"You called just before you came, and I had to make do with what I had. If there is a girl you especially want I must ask you to let me know two or three days in advance."

"I see. But what do you mean when you say she's in training?"

"She's new, and small." Old Eguchi was startled.

"She was frightened. She asked if she mightn't have someone with her. But I wouldn't want to upset you."

"Two of them? I shouldn't think that would be so bad. But

if she's so sound asleep that she might as well be dead, how can she know whether to be frightened or not?"

"Quite true. But be easy with her. She's not used to it."

"I won't do a thing."

"I understand that perfectly."

"In training?" he muttered to himself. There were strange things in the world. As usual, the woman opened the door a crack and looked inside. "She's asleep. Please, whenever you're ready." She went out.

Eguchi had another cup of tea. He lay with his head on his arm. A chilly emptiness came over him. He got up as if the effort were almost too much for him and, quietly opening the door, looked into the secret room of velvet.

The "small" girl had a small face. Her hair, disheveled as if a braid had been undone, lay over one cheek, and the palm of her hand lay over the other and down to her mouth; and so probably her face looked even smaller than it was. Childlike, she lay sleeping. Her hand lay against her face—or rather, the edge of her relaxed hand lightly touched her cheekbone, and the bent fingers lay from the bridge of her nose down over her lips. The long middle finger reached to her jaw. It was her left hand. Her right hand lay at the edge of the quilt, which the fingers gently grasped. She wore no cosmetics. Nor did it seem that she had taken any off before going to sleep.

Old Eguchi slipped in beside her. He was careful not to touch her. She did not move. But her warmth, different from the warmth of the electric blanket, enveloped him. It was like a wild and undeveloped warmth. Perhaps the smell of her hair and skin made him think so, but it was not only that.

"Sixteen or so, maybe?" he muttered to himself.

It was a house frequented by old men who could no longer use women as women; but Eguchi, on his third visit, knew that to sleep with such a girl was a fleeting consolation, the pursuit of a vanished happiness in being alive. And were there among them old men who secretly asked to sleep forever beside a girl who had been put to sleep? There seemed to be a sadness in a young girl's body that called up in an old man a longing for death. But perhaps Eguchi was, among the old men who came to the house, one of the more easily moved; and perhaps most of them but wanted to drink in the youth of girls put to sleep, to enjoy girls who would not awaken.

At his pillow there were again two white sleeping tablets. He took them up and looked at them. They bore no marks or letters to tell him what the drug might be. It was without doubt different from the drug the girl had taken. He thought of asking on his next visit for the same drug. It was not likely that the request would be granted; but how would it be to sleep a sleep as of the dead? He was much taken with the thought of sleeping a deathlike sleep beside a girl put into a sleep like death.

"A sleep like death": the words brought back a memory of a woman. Three years before, in the spring, Eguchi had brought a woman back to his hotel in Kobe. She was from a night club, and it was past midnight. He had a drink of whisky from a bottle he kept in his room and offered some to the woman. She drank as much as he. He changed to the night kimono provided by the hotel. There was none for her. He took her in his arms still in her underwear.

He was gently and aimlessly stroking her back.

She pulled herself up. "I can't sleep in these." She took off all her clothes and threw them on the chair in front of the mirror. He was surprised, but told himself that such was the way with amateurs. She was unusually docile.

"Not yet?" he asked as he pulled away from her.

"You cheat, Mr. Eguchi." She said it twice. "You cheat." But still she was quiet and docile.

The whisky had its effect, and the old man was soon asleep. A feeling that the woman was already out of the bed awoke him in the morning. She was at the mirror arranging her hair.

"You're early."

"Because I have children."

"Children?"

"Two of them. Still very small."

She hurried away before he was out of bed.

It seemed strange that she, the first slender and firm-fleshed woman he had embraced in a long while, should have two children. Hers had not been that sort of a body. Nor had it seemed likely that those breasts had nursed a child.

He opened his suitcase to take out a clean shirt, and saw that everything had been neatly put in order for him. In the course of his ten days' stay he had wadded his dirty linen and stuffed it inside, and stirred up the contents in search of something at the bottom, and tossed in gifts he had bought and received in Kobe; and the suitcase had so swelled up that it would no longer close. She had been able to look inside, and she had seen the confusion when he opened it for cigarettes. But even so, what had made her want to put it in order for him? And when had she done the work? All of his dirty underwear and the like was neatly folded. It must have taken time, even for a woman's skilled hands. Had she done it, unable to sleep herself, after Eguchi had gone to sleep?

"Well," said Eguchi, gazing at the neat suitcase. "I wonder what made her do it?"

The next evening, as promised, the woman arrived to meet

him at a Japanese restaurant. She was wearing Japanese kimono.

"You wear kimono?"

"Sometimes. But I don't imagine I look very good in it." She laughed a diffident laugh. "I had a call from my friend at about noon. She said she was shocked. She asked if it was all right."

"You told her?"

"I don't keep secrets."

They walked through the city. Eguchi bought her material for a kimono and obi, and they went back to the hotel. From the window they could see the lights of a ship in the harbor. As they stood kissing in the window, Eguchi closed the blinds and pulled the curtains. He offered whisky to the woman, but she shook her head. She did not want to lose control of herself. She sank into a deep sleep. She awoke the next morning as Eguchi was getting out of bed.

"I slept as if I were dead. I really slept as if I were dead."

She lay still, her eyes open. They were misty, washed clean.

She knew that he would be going back to Tokyo today. She had married when her husband was in the Kobe office of a foreign company. He had been in Singapore for two years now. Next month he would be back in Kobe. She had told Eguchi all this the night before. He had not known that she was married, and married to a foreigner. He had had no trouble luring her from the night club. He had gone there on the whim of a moment, and at the next table there had been two Occidental men and four Japanese women. The middle-aged woman among them was an acquaintance of Eguchi's, and she greeted him. She was apparently acting as guide for the men. When the two men got up to dance, she asked whether he would not like to dance with the other young woman. Halfway through the second dance he suggested that they go out. It was as if she were embarking on a mischievous frolic. She readily came to the hotel, and when they were in his room, Eguchi was the one who felt the greater strain.

And so it was that Eguchi had an affair with a married woman, a foreigner's wife. She had left her children with a nurse or governess, and she did not show the reticence one might expect of a married woman; and so the feeling of having misbehaved was not strong. Certain pangs of conscience lingered on all the same. But the happiness of hearing her say that she had slept as if she were dead stayed with him like youthful music. Eguchi was sixty-four at the time, the woman perhaps in her middle or late twenties. Such had been the difference in their ages that Eguchi had thought it probably his last affair with a young woman. In the course of only two nights, of a single night, indeed, the woman who had slept as if dead had become an unforgettable woman. She had written saying that when he was next in Kobe she would like to see him again. A note a month later told him that her husband had come back, but that she would like to see him again all the same. There was a similar note yet a month later. He heard no more.

"Well," old Eguchi muttered to himself. "She got herself pregnant again, with her third one. No doubt about it." It was three years later, as he lay beside a small girl who had been put into a sleep like death, that the thought came to him.

It had not come to him before. Eguchi was puzzled that it should have come now; but the more he turned it over in his mind the surer he was that it was a fact. Had she stopped writing because she was pregnant? He was on the edge of a smile. He felt calm and reposed, as if her welcoming her husband back from Singapore and then getting pregnant had washed away the impropriety. And a fond image of the woman's body came before him. It brought no stirrings of lust. The firm, smooth, tall body was like a symbol of young womanhood. Her pregnancy was but a sudden working of his imagination, but he did not doubt it to be a fact.

"Do you like me?" she had asked him at the hotel.

"Yes, I like you. That's the question all women ask."

"But . . ." She did not go on to finish the sentence.

"Aren't you going to ask what it is I like about you?"

"All right. I won't say any more."

But the question made it clear to him that he did like her. He had not forgotten it even now, three years later. The mother of three children, would she still have a body like that of a woman who had had none? Fondness for the woman flowed over him.

It was as if he had forgotten the girl beside him, the girl who had been put to sleep; but it was she who had made him think of the Kobe woman. The arm bent with the hand against the cheek was in his way. He grasped it by the wrist and stretched it out under the quilt. Too warm from the electric blanket, she had pushed it down to her shoulder blades. The small fresh roundness of the shoulders was so near as almost to brush against his eyes. He wanted to see whether he could take a shoulder in the palm of one hand, but held back. The flesh was not rich enough to hide the shoulder blades. He wanted to stroke them, but again held back. He gently brushed aside the hair over her right cheek. The sleeping face was soft in the gentle light from the ceiling and the crimson curtains. Nothing had been done to the eyebrows. The eyelashes were even, and so long that he could have taken them between his fingers. The lower lip thickened slightly toward the center. He could not see her teeth.

For Eguchi when he came to this house, there was nothing

more beautiful than a young face in dreamless sleep. Might it be called the sweetest consolation to be found in this world? No woman, however beautiful, could conceal her age when she was asleep. And even when a woman was not beautiful she was at her best asleep. Or perhaps this house chose girls whose sleeping faces were particularly beautiful. He felt his life, his troubles over the years, fade away as he gazed at the small face. It would have been a happy night had he even now taken the tablets and gone off to sleep; but he lay quietly, his eyes closed. He did not want to sleep—for the girl, having made him remember the woman in Kobe, might bring other memories too.

The thought that the young wife in Kobe, having welcomed her husband back after two years, had immediately become pregnant, and the intense feeling, as of the inevitable, that it had to be the case were not quick to leave Eguchi. It seemed to him that the affair had done nothing to sully the child the woman had carried. The pregnancy and the birth were a reality and a blessing. Young life was at work in the woman, telling him all the more of his age. But why had she quietly given herself to him, without resistance and without restraint? It was, he thought, something that had not happened before in all his near seventy years. There had been nothing in her of the whore or the profligate. He had less sense of guilt, indeed, than he now had in this house, beside the girl so strangely put to sleep. Still in bed, he had watched with pleasure and approval as the woman quietly hurried off to the small children awaiting her. Probably the last young woman in his life, she had become unforgettable, and he did not think that she would have forgotten him. Though the affair would remain a secret throughout their lives, leaving no deep cuts, he did not think that either of them would forget.

But it was strange that this small girl in training as a "sleeping beauty" should have brought back the Kobe woman so vividly. He opened his eyes. He stroked her eyelashes gently. She frowned and turned away, and her lips parted. Her tongue shrank downwards, as if withdrawing into her lower jaw. There was a pleasing hollow down the precise center of the childlike tongue. He was tempted. He peered into the open mouth. If he were to throttle her, would there be spasms along the small tongue? He remembered how, long before, he had known a prostitute even younger than this girl. His own tastes were rather different, but she was the one who had been allotted to him by his host. She used her long, thin tongue. It was watery, and Eguchi was not pleased. From the town came sounds of drum and flute that made one's heart beat faster. It seemed to be a festival night. The girl had almond eyes and a spirited face. She rushed ahead, despite the fact that she obviously had no interest in her customer.

"The festival," said Eguchi. "I imagine you're in a hurry to get to the festival."

"Why, you're exactly right. You've hit the nail on the head. I was on my way with a friend, and then I got called here."

"All right," he said, avoiding the cold, watery tongue. "Be on your way again. The drums are coming from a shrine, I suppose."

"But the woman here will scold me."

"I'll make excuses."

"You will? Really?"

"How old are you?"

"Fourteen."

She was not in the least afraid of men. There had been no suggestion of shame or fear. Her mind had been elsewhere. Scarcely putting herself in order, she hurried off to the festival.

Eguchi smoked a cigarette and listened for a time to the drums and flutes and the hawkers at the night stalls.

How old had he been? He could not remember, but even if he had been of an age that could send the girl off to the festival without regrets, he had not been the old man he was now. The girl tonight was perhaps two or three years older than the other, and her body was more a woman's. The great difference was that she had been put to sleep and would not awaken. If festival drums were echoing tonight she would not hear them.

Straining his ears, he thought he could hear a faint late-autumn wind blowing down over the hill behind the house. The warm breath from the girl's small parted lips came to his face. The dim light from the crimson velvet curtains flowed down inside her mouth. It did not seem to him that this girl's tongue would be like the other's, cold and watery. The temptation was still strong. This girl was the first of the "sleeping beauties" who had shown him her tongue. The impulse toward a misdeed more exciting than putting his finger to her tongue flashed through him.

But the misdeed did not take clear shape in Eguchi's mind as cruelty and terror. What was the very worst thing a man could do to a woman? The affairs with the Kobe woman and the fourteen-year-old prostitute, for instance, were of but a moment in a long life, and they flowed away in a moment. To marry, to rear his daughters, these things were on the surface good; but to have had the long years in his power, to have controlled their lives, to have warped their natures even, these might be evil things. Perhaps, beguiled by custom and order, one's sense of evil went numb.

Lying beside a girl who had been put to sleep was doubtless evil. The evil would become clearer were he to kill her. It would be easy to strangle her, or to cover her nose and mouth. She was asleep with her mouth open, showing her childlike tongue. It was a tongue that seemed likely to curl around his finger, were he to touch it, like that of a babe at its mother's breast. He put his hand to her jaw and upper lip and closed her mouth. When he took it away the mouth fell open again. In the lips parted in sleep, the old man saw youth.

The fact of her being so very young may have caused the impulse to flash through him; but it seemed to him that among the old men who secretly came to this "house of the sleeping beauties," there must be some who not only looked wistfully back to the vanished past but sought to forget the evil they had done through their lives. Old Kiga, who had introduced Eguchi to the house, had of course not revealed the secrets of the other guests. There were probably only a few of them. Eguchi could imagine that they were worldly successes. But among them must be some who had made their successes by wrongdoing and kept their gains by repeated wrongdoing. They would not be men at peace with themselves. They would be among the defeated, rather— victims of terror. In their hearts as they lay against the flesh of naked young girls put to sleep would be more than fear of approaching death and regret for their lost youth. There might also be remorse, and the turmoil so common in the families of the successful. They would have no Buddha before whom to kneel. The naked girl would know nothing, would not open her eyes, if one of the old men were to hold her tight in his arms, shed cold tears, even sob and wail. The old man need feel no shame, no damage to his pride. The regrets and the sadness could flow quite freely. And might not the "sleeping beauty" herself be a Buddha of sorts? And she was flesh and blood. Her young skin and scent might be forgiveness for the sad old men.

Old Eguchi quietly closed his eyes as these thoughts came to him. It seemed a little strange that, among the three "sleeping beauties" he had been with, the one tonight, the smallest and youngest, quite inexperienced, should have called them up. He took her in his arms, enveloped her. Until then he had avoided touching her. Drained of strength, she did not resist. She was pathetically slight. She may have felt Eguchi even from the depths of sleep. She closed her mouth. Her hips, thrust forward, came against him roughly.

What sort of life would she have, he wondered. Would it be a quiet and peaceful one, even though she achieved no great eminence? He hoped that she would find happiness for having given comfort to the old men here. He almost thought that, as in old legends, she was the incarnation of a Buddha. Were there not old stories in which prostitutes and courtesans were Buddhas incarnate?

He took her loose hair lightly in his hand. He strove to quiet himself, seeking confession and repentance of his misdeeds; but it was the women in his past that floated into his mind. And what he remembered fondly had nothing to do with the length of his affairs with them, their beauty, their grace and intelligence. It had to do with such things as the remark the Kobe woman had made: "I slept as if I were dead. I really slept as if I were dead." It had to do with women who had lost themselves in his caresses, who had been frantic with pleasure. Was the pleasure less a matter of the depth of their affection than of their physical endowments? What would this girl be like when she was fully grown? He extended the arm that embraced her and stroked her back. But of course he had no way of knowing. When on his previous visit he had slept with the witchlike girl, he had asked himself how much of the depth and breadth of sex he had known in his sixty-seven years, and he had felt the thought as his own senility; and it was strange that the small girl tonight seemed to bring sex back from the past. He touched his lips gently to her closed lips. There was no taste. They were dry. The fact that there was no taste seemed to improve them. He might never see her again. By the time the small lips were damp with the taste of sex, Eguchi might already be dead. The thought did not sadden him. Leaving her mouth, his lips brushed against her eyebrows and eyelashes. She moved her head slightly. Her forehead came against his eyes. His eyes were closed, and he closed them tighter.

Behind the closed eyes an endless succession of phantasms floated up and disappeared. Presently they began to take on a certain shape. A number of golden arrows flew near and passed on. At their tips were hyacinths of deep purple. At their tails were orchids of various colors. It seemed strange that at such speed the flowers did not fall. Eguchi opened his eyes. He had begun to doze off.

He had not yet taken the sleeping tablets. He looked at his watch, beside them. It was twelve-thirty. He took them in his hand. But it seemed a pity to go to sleep tonight, when he felt none of the gloom and the loneliness of old age. The girl was breathing peacefully. Whatever she had taken or had an injection of, she seemed to be in no pain. Perhaps it was a very large dose of sleeping medicine, perhaps it was a light poison. Eguchi thought that he would like at least once to sink into such a deep sleep. Getting quietly out of bed, he went to the room next door. He pressed the button, thinking to demand of the woman the medicine the girl had been given. The bell rang on and on, informing him of the cold, inside and out. He was reluctant to ring too long, here in the secret house in the depths of the night. The region was a warm one, and withered leaves still clung to the branches; but, in a wind so faint that it was scarcely a wind at all, he could hear the rustle of fallen leaves in the garden.

The waves against the cliff were gentle. The place was like a haunted house in the lonely quiet. He shivered. He had come out in a cotton kimono.

Back in the secret room, the small girl's cheeks were flushed. The electric blanket was turned low, but she was young. He warmed himself against her. Her back was arched in the warmth. Her feet were exposed.

"You'll catch cold," said Eguchi. He felt the great difference in their ages. It would have been good to take the small girl inside him.

"Did you hear me ring last night?" he asked as the woman of the house served him breakfast. "I wanted the medicine you gave her. I wanted to sleep like her."

"That's not permitted. It's dangerous for old people."

"You needn't worry. I have a strong heart. And I wouldn't have any regrets if I went."

"You're asking a lot for someone who has only been here three times."

"What is the most you can get by with in this house?"

She stared back at him, a faint smile on her lips.

4

The gray of the winter morning was by evening a cold drizzle. Inside the gate of the "house of the sleeping beauties," Eguchi noticed that the drizzle had become sleet. The usual woman closed and locked the gate behind him. He saw white dots in the light pointed at his feet. There was only a scattering of them. They were soft, and melted as they hit the flagstones.

"Be careful," said the woman. "The stones are wet." Holding an umbrella over him, she tried to take his hand. The forbidding warmth from the middle-aged hand seemed about to come through his glove.

"I'm all right." He shook her away. "I'm not so old yet that I need to be led by the hand."

"They're slippery." The fallen maple leaves had not been swept away. Some were withered and faded, but they glowed in the rain.

"Do you have them coming here half paralyzed? Do you have to lead them and hold them up?"

"You're not to ask about the others."

"But the winter must be dangerous for them. What would you do if one of them had a stroke or a heart attack?"

"That would be the end of things," she said coldly. "It might be paradise for the gentleman, of course."

"You wouldn't come through undamaged yourself."

"No." Whatever there might have been in the woman's past to account for such composure, there was no flicker of change in her expression.

The upstairs room was as usual, save that the village of the maple leaves had been changed for a snow scene. It too was without doubt a reproduction.

"You always give me such short notice," she said as she made the usual good tea. "Didn't you like any of the other three?"

"I liked all three of them too well."

"Then you should let me know two or three days in advance which you want. You're very promiscuous."

"Is it promiscuous, even with a sleeping girl? She doesn't know a thing. It could be anyone."

"She may be asleep, but she's still flesh and blood."

"Do they ever ask what sort of old man was with them?"

"They are absolutely forbidden to. That's the strict rule of the house. You needn't worry."

"I believe you suggested it wouldn't do to have a man too fond of one of your girls. Do you remember? We spoke about promiscuousness, and you said to me exactly what I said to you tonight. We've changed places. Very odd. Is the woman in you beginning to show through?"

There was a sarcastic smile at the corners of her thin lips. "I would imagine that over the years you've made a great many women weep."

"What an idea!" Eguchi was caught off balance.

"I think you protest too much."

"I wouldn't be coming here if I were that kind of man. The old men who come here still have their attachments. But struggling and moaning won't bring anything back."

"I wonder." There still was no change in her expression.

"I asked you last time. What is the worst they can get by with?"

"Having the girl asleep, I should think."

"Can I have the same medicine?"

"I believe I had to refuse you last time."

"What is the worst thing an old man can do?"

"There are no bad things in this house." She lowered her youthful voice, which seemed to impose itself upon him with a new force.

"No bad things?"

The woman's dark eyes were calm. "Of course, if you were to try to strangle one of the girls, it would be like wrenching the arm of a baby."

The remark was distasteful. "She wouldn't even wake up then?"

"I think not."

"Made to order if you wanted to commit suicide and take someone with you."

"Please do, if you feel lonely about doing it by yourself."

"And when you're too lonely even for suicide?"

"I suppose there are such times for old people." As always, her manner was calm. "Have you been drinking? You're not making a great deal of sense."

"I've had something worse than liquor."

She glanced at him briefly. "The one tonight is very warm," she said as if to make light of his words. "Just right for a cold

night like this. Warm yourself with her." And she went downstairs.

Eguchi opened the door to the secret room. The sweet smell of
woman was stronger than usual. The girl lay with her back to
him. She was breathing heavily, though not quite snoring. She
seemed to be a large girl. He could not be certain in the light from
the crimson velvet curtains, but her rich hair may have had a
reddish cast. The skin from the full ears over the round neck was
extraordinarily white. She seemed, as the woman had said, very
warm, and yet she was not flushed.

"Ah!" he cried out involuntarily as he slipped in behind her.

She was indeed warm. Her skin was so smooth that it seemed to
cling to him. From its moistness came the scent. He lay still for
a time, his eyes closed. The girl too lay still. The flesh was rich
at the hips and below. The warmth less sank into him than
enveloped him. Her bosom was full, but the breasts seemed low
and wide, and the nipples were remarkably small. The woman
had spoken of strangulation. He remembered now and trembled
at the thought, because of the girl's skin. If he were to strangle
her, what sort of scent would she give off? He forced upon himself a picture of the girl in the daytime, and, to subdue the temptation, he gave her an awkward gait. The excitement faded. But
what was awkwardness in a walking girl? What were well-
shaped legs? What, for a sixty-seven-year-old man with a girl who
was probably for the one night only, were intelligence, culture,
barbarity? He was but touching her. And, put to sleep, she
knew nothing of the fact that an ugly old man was touching her.
Nor would she know tomorrow. Was she a toy, a sacrifice?
Old Eguchi had come to this house only four times, and yet the
feeling that with each new visit there was a new numbness inside
him was especially strong tonight.

Was this girl also well trained? Perhaps because she had come to think nothing of the sad old men who were her guests, she did not respond to Eguchi's touch. Any kind of inhumanity, given practice, becomes human. All the varieties of transgression are buried in the darkness of the world. But Eguchi was a little different from the other old men who frequented the house. Indeed he was very different. Old Kiga, who had introduced him, had been wrong when he thought Eguchi like the rest of them. Eguchi had not ceased to be a man. It might therefore be said that he did not feel the sorrow and happiness, the regrets and loneliness, as intensely as the others. It was not necessary for him that the girl remain asleep.

There had been his second visit, when, with that witch of a girl, he had come close to violating the rule of the house, and had pulled himself back in his astonishment at finding that she was a virgin. He had vowed then to observe the rule, to leave the sleeping beauties in peace. He had vowed to respect the old men's secret. It did seem to be the case that all the girls of the house were virgins; and to what sort of solicitude did that attest? Was it the wish of the old men, a wish that approached the mournful? Eguchi thought he understood, and he also thought it foolish.

But he was suspicious of the one tonight. He found it hard to believe that she was a virgin. Raising his chest to her shoulder, he looked into her face. It was not as well put together as her body. But it was more innocent than he would have expected. The nostrils were somewhat distended, and the bridge of the nose was low. The cheeks were broad and round. A widow's peak came low over her forehead. The short eyebrows were heavy and regular.

"Very pretty," muttered old Eguchi, pressing his cheek to hers. It too was smooth and moist. Perhaps because his weight was heavy against her shoulder, she turned face up. Eguchi pulled away.

He lay for a time with his eyes closed, for the girl's scent was unusually strong. It is said that the sense of smell is the quickest to call up memories; but was this not too thick and sweet a smell? Eguchi thought of the milky smell of a baby. Even though the two were utterly different, were they not somehow basic to humanity? From ancient times old men had sought to use the scent given off by girls as an elixir of youth. The scent of the girl tonight could not have been called fragrant. Were he to violate the rule of the house, there would be an objectionably sharp and carnal smell. But was the fact that it came to him as objectionable a sign that Eguchi was already senile? Was not this sort of heavy, sharp smell the basis of human life? She seemed like a girl who could easily be made pregnant. Although she had been put to sleep, her physiological processes had not stopped, and she would awaken in the course of the next day. If she were to become pregnant, it would be quite without her knowledge. Suppose Eguchi, now sixty-seven, were to leave such a child behind. It was the body of woman that invited man into the lower circles of hell.

She had been stripped of all defenses, for the sake of her aged guest, of the sad old man. She was naked, and she would not awaken. Eguchi felt a wave of pity for her. A thought came to him: the aged have death, and the young have love, and death comes once, and love comes over and over again. It was a thought for which he was unprepared, but it calmed him—not that he had been especially overwrought. From outside there came the faint rustle of sleet. The sound of the sea had faded away. Old Eguchi could see the great, dark sea, on which the sleet fell and melted. A wild bird like a great eagle flew skimming the waves, something in its mouth dripping blood. Was it not a human infant? It could not be. Perhaps it was the specter of human iniquity. He shook his head gently on the pillow and the specter went away.

"Warm, warm," said Eguchi.

It was not only the electric blanket. She had thrown off the quilt, and her bosom, rich and wide but somewhat wanting in emphasis, was half exposed. The fair skin was slightly tinged in the light from the crimson velvet. Gazing at the handsome bosom, he traced the peaked hairline with his finger. She continued to breathe quietly and slowly. What sort of teeth would be behind the small lips? Taking the lower lip at its center he opened it slightly. Though not small in proportion to the size of her lips, her teeth were small all the same, and regularly ranged. He took away his hand. Her lips remained open. He could still see the tips of her teeth. He rubbed off some of the lipstick at his fingertips on the full earlobe, and the rest on the round neck. The scarcely visible smear of red was pleasant against the remarkably white skin.

Yes, she would be a virgin. Having had doubts about the girl on his second night, and having been startled at his own baseness, he felt no impulse to investigate. What was it to him? Then, as he began to think that it indeed was something to him, he seemed to hear a derisive voice.

"Is it some devil in there trying to laugh at me?"

"Nothing as simple, I'm afraid. You're making too much of your own sentimentality, and your dissatisfaction at not being able to die."

"I'm trying to think for old men who are sadder than I am."

"Scoundrel. Someone who puts the blame on others is not fit to be ranked with the scoundrels."

"Scoundrel? Very well, a scoundrel. But why is a virgin pure, and another woman not? I haven't asked for virgins."

"That's because you don't know real senility. Don't come to this place again. If by a chance in a million, a chance in a million, a girl were to open her eyes—aren't you underestimating the shame?"

Something like a self-interrogation passed through Eguchi's mind; but of course it did not establish that only virgins were put to sleep in this house. Having visited it only four times, he was puzzled that all four girls should have been virgins. Was it the demand, the hope of the old men that they should be?

If the girl should awaken—the thought had a strong pull. If she were to open her eyes, even in a daze, how intense would the shock be, of what sort would it be? She would probably not go on sleeping if, for instance, he were to cut her arm almost off or stab her in the chest or abdomen.

"You're depraved," he muttered to himself.

The impotence of the other old men was probably not very far off for Eguchi himself. Thoughts of atrocities rose in him: destroy this house, destroy his own life too, because the girl tonight was not what could have been called a regular-featured beauty, because he felt close to him a pretty girl with her broad bosom exposed. He felt something like contrition turned upon itself. And there was contrition too for a life that seemed likely to have a timid ending. He did not have the courage of his youngest daughter, with whom he had gone to see the camellia. He closed his eyes again.

Two butterflies were sporting in low shrubbery along the stepping-stones of a garden. They disappeared in the shrubbery, they brushed against it, they seemed to be enjoying themselves. They flew slightly higher and danced lightly in and out, and another butterfly appeared from the leaves, and another. Two sets of mates, he thought—and then there were five, all whirling about together. Was it a fight? But butterflies appeared one after another from the shrubbery, and the garden was a dancing swarm of white butterflies, close to the ground. The down-swept branches of a maple waved in a wind that did not seem to exist. The twigs were delicate and, because the leaves were large, sensitive to the wind. The swarm of butterflies had so grown that it was like a field of white flowers. The maple leaves here had quite fallen. A few shriveled leaves might still be clinging to the branches, but tonight it was sleeting.

Eguchi had forgotten the cold of the sleet. Was that dancing swarm of white butterflies brought by the ample white bosom of the girl, spread out here beside him? Was there something in the girl to quiet the bad impulses in an old man? He opened his eyes. He gazed at the small pink nipples. They were like a symbol of good. He put a cheek to them. The back of his eyelids seemed to warm. He wanted to leave his mark on the girl. If he were to violate the rule of the house, she would be in dismay when she awoke. He left on her breasts several marks the color of blood. He shivered.

"You'll be cold." He pulled up the quilt. He drank down both of the tablets at his pillow. "A bit heavy in the lower parts." He reached down and pulled her toward him.

The next morning he was twice aroused by the woman of the house. The first time she rapped on the door.

"It's nine o'clock, sir."

"I'm getting up. I imagine it's cold out there."

"I lit the stove early."

"What about the sleet?"

"It's cloudy, but the sleet has stopped."

"Oh?"

"I've had your breakfast ready for some time."

"I see." With this indifferent answer, he closed his eyes again. "A devil will be coming for you," he said. He brought himself against the remarkable skin of the girl.

In no more than ten minutes the woman had come again.

"Sir!" This time she rapped sharply. "Are you back in bed?" Her voice too was sharp.

"The door isn't locked," he said. The woman came in. Sluggishly, he pulled himself up. She helped him into his clothes. She even put on his socks, but her touch was unpleasant. In the next room the tea was, as always, good. As he sipped at it, she turned a cold, suspicious eye on him.

"And how was she? Did you like her?"

"Well enough, I suppose."

"That's good. And did you have pleasant dreams?"

"Dreams? None at all. I just slept. It's been a long time since I slept so well." He yawned openly. "I'm still not wide awake."

"I imagine you were tired last night."

"It was her fault. Does she come here often?"

The woman looked down, her expression severe.

"I have a special request," he said. His manner was serious. "When I've finished breakfast, will you let me have some more sleeping medicine? I'll pay extra. Not that I know when the girl will wake up."

"Completely out of the question." The woman's face had taken on a muddy pallor, and her shoulders were rigid. "You're really going too far."

"Too far?" He tried to laugh, but the laugh refused to come.

Perhaps suspecting that Eguchi had done something to the girl, she went hastily into the next room.

5

The new year came, the wild sea was of dead winter. On land there was little wind.

"It was good of you to come on such a cold night." At the house of the sleeping beauties, the woman opened the door.

"That's why I've come," said old Eguchi. "To die on a night like this, with a young girl's skin to warm him—that would be paradise for an old man."

"You say such pleasant things."

"An old man lives next door to death."

A stove was burning in the usual upstairs room. And as usual the tea was good.

"I feel a draft."

"Oh?" She looked around. "There shouldn't be any."

"Do we have a ghost with us?"

She started and looked at him. Her face was white.

"Give me another cup. A full one. Don't cool it. Let me have it off the fire."

She did as ordered. "Have you heard something?" she asked in a cold voice.

"Maybe."

"Oh? You heard and still you've come?" Sensing that Eguchi had heard, she had evidently decided not to hide the secret; but her expression was forbidding. "I shouldn't, I know, after having brought you all this distance—but may I ask you to leave?"

"I came with my eyes open."

She laughed. One could hear something diabolical in the laugh.

"It was bound to happen. Winter is a dangerous time for old men. Maybe you should close down in winter."

She did not answer.

"I don't know what sort of old men come here, but if another dies and then another, you'll be in trouble."

"Tell it to the man who owns the place. What have I done wrong?" Her face was ashen.

"Oh, but you did do something wrong. It was still dark, and they took the body to an inn. I imagine you helped."

She clutched at her knees. "It was for his sake. For his good name."

"Good name? The dead have good names? But you're right. It's stupid, but I imagine things do have to be patched over. More for the sake of the family. Does the owner of this place have the inn too?"

The woman did not answer.

"I doubt if the newspapers would have had much to say, even if he did die beside a naked girl. If I'd been that old man, I think I'd have been happier left as I was."

"There would have been investigations, and the room itself is a little strange, you know, and the other gentlemen who are good enough to come here might have had questions asked. And then there are the girls."

"I imagine the girl would sleep on without knowing the old man had died. He might toss about a little, but I doubt if that would be enough to wake her up."

"But if we had left him here, then we'd have had to carry the girl out and hide her. And even then they'd have known that a woman had been with him."

"You'd take her away?"

"And that would be too clear a crime."

"I don't suppose she'd wake up just because an old man went cold beside her."

"I suppose not."

"So she didn't even know he was dead." How long after the old man died had the girl, put to sleep, lain warming the corpse? She had not known when the body was carried away.

"My blood pressure is good and my heart is strong and you have nothing to worry about. But if it should happen to me, I must ask you not to carry me away. Leave me here beside her."

"Quite out of the question," said the woman hastily. "I must ask you to leave if you insist upon saying such things."

"I'm joking." He could not think that sudden death might be near.

The newspaper notice of the funeral had but mentioned "sudden death." The details had been whispered to Eguchi at the funeral by old Kiga. The cause of death had been heart failure.

"It wasn't the sort of inn for a company director to be found in," said Kiga, "and there was another he often stayed at. And so people said that old Fukura must have died a happy death. Not of course that they know what really happened."

"Oh?"

"A kind of euthanasia, you might say. But not the real thing. More painful. We were very close, and I guessed immediately, and went to investigate. But I haven't told anyone. Not even the family knows. Do those notices in the newspapers amuse you?"

There were two notices side by side, the first over the names of his wife and son, the other over that of his company.

"Fukura was like this, you know." Kiga's gestures indicated a thick neck, a thick chest, and especially a large paunch. "You'd better be careful yourself."

"You needn't worry about me."

"And they carried that huge body away in the night."

Who had carried him away? Someone in an automobile, no doubt. The picture was not a pleasant one.

"They seem to have gotten away with it," whispered old Kiga at the funeral, "but with this sort of thing going on, I doubt if that house will last long."

"Probably not."

Tonight, sensing that Eguchi knew of old Fukura's death, the woman of the house made no attempt to hide the secret; but she was being careful.

"And the girl really knew nothing about it?" Eguchi was unnecessarily persistent.

"There would be no way for her to know. But he seems to have been in pain. There was a scratch from her neck over her breast. She of course did not know what had happened. 'What a nasty old man,' she said when she woke up the next morning."

"A nasty old man. Even in his last struggles."

"It was nothing you could call a wound, really. Just a welt with blood oozing out in places."

She now seemed prepared to tell him everything. He no

longer wanted to hear. The victim was but an old man who had been meant to drop dead somewhere some day. Perhaps it had been a happy death. Eguchi's imagination played with the picture of that huge body being carried to the hot spring inn.

"The death of an old man is an ugly thing. I suppose you might think of it as rebirth in heaven—but I'm sure he went the other way."

She had no comment.

"Do I know the girl who was with him?"

"That I cannot tell you."

"I see."

"She will be on holiday till the welt goes away."

"Another cup of tea, please. I'm thirsty."

"Certainly. I'll change the leaves."

"You managed to keep it quiet. But don't you suppose you'll be closing down before long?"

"Do you think so?" Her manner was calm. She did not look up from the tea. "The ghost should be coming out one of these nights."

"I'd like to have a good talk with it."

"And what about?"

"About sad old men."

"I was joking."

He took a sip of tea.

"Yes, of course. You were joking. But I have a ghost here inside me. You have one too." He pointed at the woman with his right hand. "How did you know he was dead?"

"I heard a strange groaning and came upstairs. His breathing and his pulse had stopped."

"And the girl didn't know," he said again.

"We arrange things so nothing as minor as that will wake her."

"As minor as that? And she didn't know when you carried the body out?"

"No."

"So the girl is the awful one."

"Awful? What is awful about her? Stop this talk and go on into the other room. Have any of the other girls seemed awful?"

"Maybe youth is awful for an old man."

"And what does that mean?" Smiling faintly, she got up, went to the cedar door, opened it a crack, and looked in. "Fast asleep. Here. Here." She took the key from her obi. "I meant to tell you. There are two of them."

"Two?" Eguchi was startled. Perhaps the girls knew of the death of old Fukura.

"You may go in whenever you're ready." The woman left.

The curiosity and the shyness of his first visit had left him. Yet he pulled back as he opened the door.

Was this also an apprentice? But she seemed wild and rough, quite unlike the "small girl" of the other night. The wildness made him almost forget about the death of old Fukura. It was the girl who had been put to sleep nearer the door. Perhaps because she was not used to such devices for the aged as electric blankets, or perhaps because her warmth kept the winter cold at a distance, she had pushed the bedding down to the pit of her stomach. She seemed to be lying with her legs spread wide. She lay face up, her arms flung out. The nipples were large and dark, and had a purplish cast. It was not a beautiful color in the light from the crimson velvet curtains. Nor could the skin of the neck and breasts have been called beautiful. Still it had a dark glow. There seemed to be a faint odor at the armpits.

"Life itself," muttered Eguchi. A girl like this breathed life into a sixty-seven-year-old man. Eguchi had doubts as to whether the girl was Japanese. She could not yet be twenty, for the nipples were flat despite the width of the breasts. The body was firm.

He took her hand. The fingers and the nails were long. She would be tall, in the modern fashion. What sort of voice would she have, what would be her way of speaking? There were numbers of women on radio and television whose voices he liked. He would close his eyes and listen to them. He wanted to hear this girl's voice. There was of course no way of really talking to a girl who was asleep. How could he make her speak? A voice was different when it came from a sleeping person. Most women have several voices, but this girl would probably have only one. Even from the sleeping form he could see that she was untutored and without affectation.

He sat toying with the long fingernails. Were fingernails so hard? Were these healthy young fingernails? The color of blood was vivid beneath them. He noticed for the first time that she had on a golden necklace thin as a thread. He wanted to smile. Although she had pushed the bedding down below her breasts on so cold a night, there seemed to be a touch of perspiration at her forehead. He took a handkerchief from his pocket and wiped it away. The scent was strong on the handkerchief. He also wiped her armpits. Since he would not be able to take the handkerchief home, he wadded it and threw it into a corner of the room.

"She has on lipstick." It was most natural that she should, but with this girl the lipstick too made him want to smile. He gazed at it for a time. "Has she had an operation for a harelip?"

He retrieved his handkerchief and wiped at her lipstick. There was no trace of surgery. The center of the upper lip was raised, to cut a clean pointed line. It was strangely appealing.

He remembered a kiss from more than forty years before. With his hands very lightly on the shoulders of the girl before him, he had brought his lips to hers. She shook her head left and right.

"No, no. I don't."

"You have."

"No, no. I don't."

Eguchi wiped his lips, and showed her the handkerchief stained pink.

"But you have. Look at this."

The girl took the handkerchief and stared at it, and then stuffed it into her handbag.

"I don't," she said, hanging her head silently, choked with tears.

They had not met again. And what might she have done with the handkerchief? But more than the handkerchief, what of the girl herself? Was she still living, now more than forty years later?

How many years had he forgotten her, until she was brought back by the peaked upper lip of the girl who had been put to sleep? There was lipstick on the handkerchief, and the girl's had been wiped away; and would she think, if he left it by her pillow, that he had stolen a kiss? The guests here were of course free to kiss. Kissing was not among the forbidden acts. A man could kiss, however senile he was. The girl would not avoid him, and she would never know. The sleeping lips might be cold and wet. Do not the dead lips of a woman one has loved give the greater thrill of emotion? The urge was not strong with Eguchi, as he thought of the bleak senility of the old men who frequented the house.

Yet the unusual shape of these lips did arouse him. So there are such lips, he thought, lightly touching the center of the upper lip with his little finger. It was dry. And the skin seemed thick. The girl began licking her lip, and did not stop until it was well moistened. He took his finger away.

"Does she kiss even when she's asleep?"

He stopped, however, at briefly stroking the hair at her ear. It was coarse and stiff. He got up and undressed.

"You'll catch cold. I don't care how healthy you are." He put her arms under the bedding and covered her breasts. He lay down beside her. She turned over. Then, with a groan, she thrust her arms abruptly out. The old man was pushed cleanly away. He laughed on and on. A most valiant sort of apprentice, he said to himself.

Because she had been put into a sleep from which she would not awaken, and because her body was probably numbed, he could do as he wished; but the vigor to take such a girl by force was no longer in Eguchi—or he had long forgotten it. He approached her with a soft passion, a gentle affirmation, a feeling of nearness to woman. The adventure, the fight that set one to breathing harder, had gone.

"I am old," he muttered, thinking such thoughts even while smiling at his rejection by the sleeping girl.

He was not really qualified to come to this house as the other old men came. But it was probably the girl with the darkly glowing skin who made him feel more keenly than usual that he too had left before him not a great deal of life as a man.

It seemed to him that to force himself upon the girl would be the tonic to bring stirrings of youth. He was growing a little tired of the "house of the sleeping beauties." And even as he wearied of it the number of his visits increased. He felt a sudden urging of the blood: he wanted to use force on her, break the rule of the house, destroy the ugly nostrum, and so take his leave. But force would not be necessary. There would be no resistance from the body of the girl put to sleep. He could probably even strangle her with no difficulty. The impulse left him, and an emptiness, dark in its depths, spread over him. The high waves were near and seemed a great distance away, partly because here on the land there was no wind. He saw the dark floor of the night of the dark sea. Raising himself on an elbow, he brought his face to the girl's. She was breathing heavily. He decided not to kiss her, and fell back again.

He lay as she had thrust him away, his chest exposed. He went to the other girl. She had been facing away, but she rolled over toward him. There was a gentle voluptuousness in this greeting, even as she lay asleep. One hand fell at the old man's hip.

"A good combination." Toying with the girl's fingers, he closed his eyes. The small-boned fingers were supple, so supple that it seemed they would bend indefinitely without breaking. He wanted to take them in his mouth. Her breasts were small but round and high. They fitted into the palm of his hand. The roundness at her hips was similar. Woman is infinite, thought the old man, with a touch of sadness. He opened his eyes. She had a long neck. It too was slender and graceful. But the slenderness was different from that of old Japan. There was a double line at the closed eyelids, so shallow that with the eyes open it might become but a single line. Or it might be at times single and at times double. Or perhaps a single line at one eye and a double line at the other. Because of the light from the velvet curtains he could not be sure of the color of her skin; but it seemed tan at the face, white at the neck, somewhat tan again at the shoulders, and so white at the breasts that it might have been bleached.

He could see that the darkly glowing girl was tall. This one did not seem to be much shorter. He stretched out a leg. His toes first came against the thick-skinned sole of the dark girl's foot. It was oily. He drew his foot away hastily, but the withdrawal became an invitation. The thought flashed through his mind that old Fukura's partner when he had his last seizure had been this dark-skinned girl. Hence tonight there were two girls.

But that could not be the case. The girl who had been with Fukura was on vacation until the welt over her neck and breast went away. Had the woman of the house not just this moment told him so? He again put his foot against the thick-skinned sole of the girl's foot, and explored the dark flesh upwards.

A spasm came over to him, as if to say: "Initiate me into the spell of life." The girl had pushed off the quilt, or rather the electric blanket beneath it. One foot lay flung outside the quilt. Thinking he would like to roll her out into the midwinter cold, he gazed at her breasts and abdomen. He put his head to a breast and listened to her heart. He had expected it to be strong, but it was engagingly subdued. But was it not a little uneven?

"You'll catch cold." He covered her, and turned off her side of the blanket. The spell that was a woman's life, he thought, was not so great a thing. Suppose he were to throttle her. It would be easy. It would be no trouble at all even for an old man. He took his handkerchief and wiped the cheek that had been against her breast. The girl's oily smell seemed to come from it. The sound of the girl's heart stayed on, deep in his ear. He put a hand to his own heart. Perhaps because it was his own, it seemed the stronger of the two.

He turned to the gentler girl, his back toward the dark one. The well-shaped nose seemed the more courtly and elegant to his farsighted old eyes. He could not resist putting his hand under the long, slender neck and pulling her toward him. As her head moved softly toward him there came with it a sweet scent.

It mixed with the wild, sharp scent of the dark girl behind him. He brought the fair girl against him. Her breathing was short and rapid. But he need not fear that she would awaken. He lay still for a time.

"Shall I ask her to forgive me? As the last woman in my life?" The girl behind him seemed to seek to arouse him. He put out his hand and felt. The flesh there was as at her breasts.

"Be quiet. Listen to the winter waves and be quiet." He sought to calm himself.

"These girls have been put to sleep. They might as well be paralyzed. They have been given some poison or some strong drug." And why? "Why if not for money?" Yet he found himself hesitating. Every woman was different from every other. He knew that; and yet was the one before him so very different that he was ready to inflict upon her a wound that would not heal, a sorrow to last through her life? The sixty-seven-year-old Eguchi could, if he wished, think that all women's bodies were alike. And in this girl there was neither affirmation nor denial, there was no response whatsoever. All that distinguished her from a corpse was that she breathed and had warm blood. Indeed tomorrow morning when the living girl awoke, would she be much different from an open-eyed corpse? There was now in the girl no love or shame or fear. When she awoke there could remain bitterness and regret. She would not know who had taken her. She could but infer that it was an old man. She would probably not tell the woman of the house. She would conceal to the end the fact that the rule of this house of old men had been broken, and so no one would know but herself. Her soft skin clung to Eguchi. The dark girl, perhaps after all chilly now that her side of the blanket had been turned off, pressed against Eguchi with her naked back. One of her feet was between the feet of the fair-skinned girl. Eguchi felt his strength leave him—and again he wanted to laugh. He reached for the sleeping medicine. He was sandwiched tightly between them and could move only with difficulty. His hand on the fair girl's forehead, he looked at the usual tablets.

"Shall I go without them tonight?" he muttered.

It was clearly a strong drug. He would drop effortlessly into sleep. For the first time it occurred to him to wonder whether all the old men who came to the house obediently took the medicine. But was it not compounding the ugliness of old age if, regretting the hours lost in sleep, they refrained from taking it? He thought that he himself had not yet entered into that companionship of ugliness. Once again he drank down the medicine. He had once said, he remembered, that he wanted the drug the girl had taken. The woman had answered that it was dangerous for old men. He had not insisted.

Did "dangerous" suggest dying in one's sleep? Eguchi was but an old man of ordinary circumstances. Being human, he fell from time to time into a lonely emptiness, a cold despondency. Would this not be a most desirable place to die? To arouse curiosity, to invite the disdain of the world—would these not be to cap his life with a proper death? All of his acquaintances would be surprised. He could not calculate the injury he would do to his family; but to die in his sleep between, for instance, the two young girls tonight—might that not be the ultimate wish of a man in his last years? No, it was not so. Like old Fukura, he would be carried off to a miserable hot spring inn, and people would be told that he had committed suicide from an overdose of sleeping medicine. Since there would be no suicide note, it would be said that he had been despondent about the prospects ahead. He could see the faint smile of the woman of the house.

"Foolish ideas. As if I wanted to bring on bad luck."

He laughed, but it was not a bright laugh. The drug was taking effect.

"All right," he muttered. "I'll get her up and make her give me what they had."

But it was not likely that she would agree. And Eguchi was not eager to get up, and did not really want the other drug. He lay face up and put his arms around the two girls, around a soft, docile, fragrant neck, and a hard, oily neck. Something flowed up inside him. He looked at the crimson curtains to the left and the right.

"Ah."

"Ah!" It was the dark girl who seemed to answer. She put an arm on his chest. Was she in pain? He took away his arm and turned his back to her. With the free arm he embraced the hollow at the hips of the fair girl. He closed his eyes.

"The last woman in my life? Why must I think so? Even for a minute." And who had been the first woman in his life?

He was less sleepy than dazed.

The thought flashed across his mind: the first woman in his life had been his mother. "Of course. Could it be anyone except Mother?" came the unexpected affirmation. "But can I say that Mother was my woman?"

Now at sixty-seven, as he lay between two naked girls, a new truth came from deep inside him. Was it blasphemy, was it yearning? He opened his eyes and blinked, as if to drive away a nightmare. But the drug was working. He had a dull headache. Drowsily, he pursued the image of his mother; and then he sighed, and took two breasts, one of each of the girls, in the palms of his hands. A smooth one and an oily one. He closed his eyes.

Eguchi's mother had died one winter night when he was

seventeen. Eguchi and his father held her hands. She had long suffered from tuberculosis and her arms were skin and bones, but her grip was so strong that Eguchi's fingers ached. The coldness of her hand sank all the way to his shoulder. The nurse who had been massaging her feet left quietly. She had probably gone to call the doctor.

"Yoshio. Yoshio." His mother called out in little gasps. Eguchi understood, and stroked her tormented bosom. As he did so she vomited a large quantity of blood. It came bubbling from her nose. She stopped breathing. The gauze and the towels at her pillow were not enough to wipe up the blood.

"Wipe it with your sleeve, Yoshio," said his father. "Nurse, nurse! Bring a basin and water. Yes, and a new pillow and a nightgown and sheets."

It was natural that when old Eguchi thought of his mother as the first woman in his life, he thought too of her death.

"Ah!" The curtains that walled the secret room seemed the color of blood. He closed his eyes tight, but that red would not disappear. He was half asleep from the drug. The fresh young breasts of the two girls were in the palms of his two hands. His conscience and his reason were numbed, and there seemed to be tears at the corners of his eyes.

Why, in a place like this, had he thought of his mother as the first woman in his life? But the thought of his mother as his first woman did not bring up thoughts of later women. Actually his first woman had been his wife. Very well; but his old wife, having sent her three daughters out in marriage, would be sleeping alone this cold winter night. Or would she still be awake? She would not hear the sound of waves, but the cold of the night would be harsher than here. He asked himself what they were, the two breasts in his hands. They would still be coursing with warm blood when he himself was dead. And what did that fact mean? He put a certain sluggish strength into his hands. There was no response, for the breasts too were deep in sleep. When, in her last hour, he had stroked his mother's bosom, he had of course felt her withered breasts. They had not been like breasts. He did not remember them now. What he remembered was groping for them and going to sleep, one day when he was still an infant.

Old Eguchi was finally being pulled into sleep. He brought his hands from the girls' breasts into a more comfortable position. He turned toward the dark girl, because hers was the strong scent. Her rough breath hit his face. Her mouth was slightly open.

"A crooked tooth. A pretty one." He took it between his fingers. She had large teeth, but this one was small. Had her breath not been coming at him, Eguchi might have kissed the tooth. The strong scent interfered with his sleep, and he turned away. Even then her breath hit the nape of his neck. She was not snoring, but she seemed to put her voice into her breathing. He hunched his shoulders and brought his cheek to the forehead of the fair girl. She was perhaps frowning, but it also seemed that she was smiling. The oily skin of the dark girl was unpleasant behind him. It was cold and slippery. He fell asleep.

It may have been because he had difficulty sleeping between the two girls that Eguchi had a succession of nightmares. There was no thread running through them, but they were disturbingly erotic. In the last of them he came home from his honeymoon to find flowers like red dahlias blooming and waving in such profusion that they almost buried the house. Wondering whether it was the right house, he hesitated to go inside.

"Welcome home. Why are you standing there?" It was his dead mother who greeted them. "Is your wife afraid of us?"

"But the flowers, Mother?"

"Yes," said his mother calmly. "Come on in."

"I thought we had come to the wrong house. I could hardly have made a mistake. But what flowers!"

Ceremonial food had been laid out for them. After she had exchanged greetings with his bride, Eguchi's mother went into the kitchen to warm the soup. He smelled sea bream. He went out to look at the flowers. His bride went with him.

"Aren't they beautiful," she said.

"Yes." Not wishing to frighten her, he did not add that they had not been there before.

He gazed at a particularly large one among them. A red drop oozed from one of the petals.

Old Eguchi awoke with a groan. He shook his head, but he was still in a daze. He was facing the dark girl. Her body was cold. He started up. She was not breathing. He felt her breast. There was no pulse. He leaped up. He staggered and fell. Trembling violently, he went into the next room. The call button was in the alcove. He heard footsteps below.

"Did I strangle her in my sleep?" He went, almost crawled, back to the other room and looked at the girl.

"Is something wrong?" The woman of the house came in.

"She's dead." His teeth were chattering.

The woman rubbed her eyes and looked calmly down at the girl. "Dead? There's no reason that she should be."

"She's dead. She's not breathing and there's no pulse."

Her expression changing, the woman knelt beside the dark girl.

"Dead, isn't she?"

The woman rolled back the bedding and inspected the girl. "Did you do anything to her?"

"Not a thing."

"She's not dead," she said with forced coolness. "You needn't worry."

"She's dead. Call a doctor."

The woman did not answer.

"What did you give her? Maybe she was allergic."

"Don't be alarmed. We won't cause you any trouble. We won't tell your name."

"She's dead."

"I think not."

"What time is it?"

"After four."

She staggered as she lifted the dark, naked body.

"Let me help you."

"Don't bother. There's a man downstairs."

"She's heavy."

"Please. You needn't bother. Go on back to sleep. There is the other girl."

There was another girl—no remark had ever struck him more sharply. There was of course the fair-skinned girl still asleep in the next room.

"Do you expect me to sleep after this?" His voice was angry, but there was also fear in it. "I'm going home."

"Please don't. It wouldn't do to be noticed at this hour."

"I can't possibly go back to sleep."

"I'll bring you more medicine."

He heard her dragging the dark girl downstairs. Standing in his night kimono, he for the first time felt the cold press upon him. The woman came back with two white tablets.

"Here you are. Sleep late tomorrow."

"Oh?" He opened the door to the next room. The covers

were as they had been, thrown back in confusion, and the naked form of the fair girl lay in shining beauty.

He gazed at her.

He heard an automobile pulling away, probably with the dark girl's body. Was she being taken to the dubious inn to which old Fukura had been taken?

One Arm

One Arm

"I can let you have one of my arms for the night," said the girl. She took off her right arm at the shoulder and, with her left hand, laid it on my knee.

"Thank you." I looked at my knee. The warmth of the arm came through.

"I'll put the ring on. To remind you that it's mine." She smiled and raised her left arm to my chest. "Please." With but one arm, it was difficult for her to take the ring off.

"An engagement ring?"

"No. A keepsake. From my mother."

It was silver, set with small diamonds.

"Perhaps it does look like an engagement ring, but I don't mind. I wear it, and then when I take it off it's as if I were leaving my mother."

Raising the arm on my knee, I removed the ring and slipped it on the ring finger.

"Is this the one?"

"Yes." She nodded. "It will seem artificial unless the elbow and fingers bend. You won't like that. Let me make them bend for you."

She took her right arm from my knee and pressed her lips gently to it. Then she pressed them to the finger joints.

"Now they'll move."

"Thank you." I took the arm back. "Do you suppose it will speak? Will it speak to me?"

"It only does what an arm does. If it talks I'll be afraid to have it back. But try anyway. It should at least listen to what you say, if you're good to it."

"I'll be good to it."

"I'll see you again," she said, touching the right arm with her left hand, as if to infuse it with a spirit of its own. "You're his, but just for the night."

As she looked at me she seemed to be fighting back tears.

"I don't suppose you'll try to change it for your own arm," she said. "But it will be all right. Go ahead, do."

"Thank you."

I put her arm in my raincoat and went out into the foggy streets. I feared I might be thought odd if I took a taxi or a streetcar. There would be a scene if the arm, now separated from the girl's body, were to cry out, or to weep.

I held it against my chest, toward the side, my right hand on the roundness at the shoulder joint. It was concealed by the raincoat, and I had to touch the coat from time to time with my left hand to be sure that the arm was still there. Probably I was making sure not of the arm's presence but of my own happiness.

She had taken off the arm at the point I liked. It was plump and round—was it at the top of the arm or the beginning of the shoulder? The roundness was that of a beautiful Occidental girl, rare in a Japanese. It was in the girl herself, a clean, elegant roundness, like a sphere glowing with a faint, fresh light. When the girl was no longer clean that gentle roundness would fade, grow flabby. Something that lasted for a brief moment in the life of a beautiful girl, the roundness of the arm made me feel the roundness of her body. Her breasts would not be large. Shy, only large enough to cup in the hands, they would have a clinging softness and strength. And in the roundness of the arm I could feel her legs as she walked along. She would carry them lightly, like a small bird, or a butterfly moving from flower to flower. There would be the same subtle melody in the tip of her tongue when she kissed.

It was the season for changing to sleeveless dresses. The girl's shoulder, newly bared, had the color of skin not used to the raw touch of the air. It had the glow of a bud moistened in the shelter of spring and not yet ravaged by summer. I had that morning bought a magnolia bud and put it in a glass vase; and the roundness of the girl's arm was like the great, white bud. Her dress was cut back more radically than most sleeveless dresses. The joint at the shoulder was exposed, and the shoulder itself. The dress, of dark green silk, almost black, had a soft sheen. The girl was in the rounded slope of the shoulders, which drew a gentle wave with the swelling of the back. Seen obliquely from behind, the flesh from the round shoulders to the long, slender neck came to an abrupt halt at the base of the upswept hair, and the black hair seemed to cast a glowing shadow over the roundness of the shoulders.

She had sensed that I thought her beautiful, and so she lent me her right arm for the roundness there at the shoulder.

Carefully hidden under my raincoat, the girl's arm was

colder than my hand. I was giddy from the racing of my heart, and I knew that my hand would be hot. I wanted the warmth to stay as it was, the warmth of the girl herself. And the slight coolness in my hand passed on to me the pleasure of the arm. It was like her breasts, not yet touched by a man.

The fog yet thicker, the night threatened rain, and wet my uncovered hair. I could hear a radio speaking from the back room of a closed pharmacy. It announced that three planes unable to land in the fog had been circling the airport for a half hour. It went on to draw the attention of listeners to the fact that on damp nights clocks were likely to go wrong, and that on such nights the springs had a tendency to break if wound too tight. I looked for the lights of the circling planes, but could not see them. There was no sky. The pressing dampness invaded my ears, to give a wet sound like the wriggling of myriads of distant earthworms. I stood before the pharmacy awaiting further admonitions. I learned that on such nights the fierce beasts in the zoo, the lions and tigers and leopards and the rest, roared their resentment at the dampness, and that we were now to hear it. There was a roaring like the roaring of the earth. I then learned that pregnant women and despondent persons should go to bed early on such nights, and that women who applied perfume directly to their skins would find it difficult to remove afterwards.

At the roaring of the beasts, I moved off, and the warning about perfume followed me. That angry roaring had unsettled me, and I moved on lest my uneasiness be transmitted to the girl's arm. The girl was neither pregnant nor despondent, but it seemed to me that tonight, with only one arm, she should take the advice of the radio and go quietly to bed. I hoped that she would sleep peacefully.

As I started across the street I pressed my left hand against my raincoat. A horn sounded. Something brushed my side, and I twisted away. Perhaps the arm had been frightened by the horn. The fingers were clenched.

"Don't worry," I said. "It was a long way off. It couldn't see. That's why it honked."

Because I was holding something important to me, I had looked in both directions. The sound of the horn had been so far away that I had thought it must be meant for someone else. I looked in the direction from which it came, but could see no one. I could see only the headlights. They widened into a blur of faint purple. A strange color for headlights. I stood on the curb when I had crossed and watched it pass. A young woman in vermilion was driving. It seemed to me that she turned toward me and bowed. I wanted to run off, fearing that the girl had come for her arm. Then I remembered that she would hardly be able to drive with only one. But had not the woman in the car seen what I was carrying? Had she not sensed it with a woman's intuition? I would have to take care not to encounter another of the sex before I reached my apartment. The rear lights were also a faint purple. I still did not see the car. In the ashen fog a lavender blur floated up and moved away.

"She is driving for no reason, for no reason at all except to be driving. And while she drives she will simply disappear," I muttered to myself. "And what was that sitting in the back seat?"

Nothing, apparently. Was it because I went around carrying girls' arms that I felt so unnerved by emptiness? The car she drove carried the clammy night fog. And something about her had turned it faintly purple in the headlights. If not from her own body, whence had come that purplish light? Could the arm I concealed have so clothed in emptiness a woman driving alone on such a night? Had she nodded at the girl's arm from her car? Perhaps on such a night there were angels and ghosts abroad protecting women. Perhaps she had ridden not in a car but in a purple light. Her drive had not been empty. She had spied out my secret.

I made my way back to my apartment without further encounters. I stood listening outside the door. The light of a firefly skimmed over my head and disappeared. It was too large and too strong for a firefly. I recoiled backwards. Several more lights like fireflies skimmed past. They disappeared even before the heavy fog could suck them in. Had a will-o'-the-wisp, a death-fire of some sort, run on ahead of me, to await my return? But then I saw that it was a swarm of small moths. Catching the light at the door, the wings of the moths glowed like fireflies. Too large to be fireflies, and yet, for moths, so small as to invite the mistake.

Avoiding the automatic elevator, I made my way stealthily up the narrow stairs to the third floor. Not being left-handed, I had difficulty unlocking the door. The harder I tried the more my hand trembled—as if in terror after a crime. Something would be waiting for me inside the room, a room where I lived in solitude; and was not the solitude a presence? With the girl's arm I was no longer alone. And so perhaps my own solitude waited there to intimidate me.

"Go on ahead," I said, taking out the girl's arm when at length I had opened the door. "Welcome to my room. I'll turn on the light."

"Are you afraid of something?" the arm seemed to say. "Is something here?"

"You think there might be?"

"I smell something."

"Smell? It must be me that you smell. Don't you see traces of my shadow, up there in the darkness? Look carefully. Maybe my shadow was waiting for me to come back."

"It's a sweet smell."

"Ah—the magnolia," I answered brightly. I was glad it was not the moldy smell of my loneliness. A magnolia bud befitted my winsome guest. I was getting used to the dark. Even in pitch blackness I knew where everything was.

"Let me turn on the light." Coming from the arm, a strange remark. "I haven't been in your room before."

"Thank you. I'll be very pleased. No one but me has ever turned on the lights here before."

I held the arm to the switch by the door. All five lights went on at once: at the ceiling, on the table, by the bed, in the kitchen, in the bathroom. I had not thought they could be so bright.

The magnolia was in enormous bloom. That morning it had been in bud. It could have only just bloomed, and yet there were stamens on the table. Curious, I looked more closely at the stamens than at the white flower. As I picked up one or two and gazed at them, the girl's arm, laid on the table, began to move, the fingers like spanworms, and gathered the stamens in its hand. I went to throw them in the wastebasket.

"What a strong smell. It sinks right into my skin. Help me."

"You must be tired. It wasn't an easy trip. Suppose you rest awhile."

I laid the arm on the bed and sat down beside it. I stroked it gently.

"How pretty. I like it." The arm would be speaking of the bed cover. Flowers were printed in three colors on an azure ground, somewhat lively for a man who lived alone. "So this is where we spend the night. I'll be very quiet."

"Oh?"

"I'll be beside you and not beside you." *We know the feeling —*

The hand took mine gently. The nails, carefully polished, were a faint pink. The tips extended well beyond the fingers.

Against my own short, thick nails, hers possessed a strange beauty, as if they belonged to no human creature. With such fingertips, a woman perhaps transcended mere humanity. Or did she pursue womanhood itself? A shell luminous from the pattern inside it, a petal bathed in dew—I thought of the obvious likenesses. Yet I could think of no shell or petal whose color and shape resembled them. They were the nails on the girl's fingers, comparable to nothing else. More translucent than a delicate shell, than a thin petal, they seemed to hold a dew of tragedy. Every day and every night her energies were poured into the polishing of this tragic beauty. It penetrated my solitude. Perhaps my yearning, my solitude, transformed them into dew.

I rested her little finger on the index finger of my free hand, gazing at the long, narrow nail as I rubbed it with my thumb. My finger touched the tip of hers, sheltered by the nail. The finger bent, and the elbow too.

"Does it tickle?" I asked. "It must."

I had spoken carelessly. I knew that the tips of a woman's fingers were sensitive when the nails were long. And so I had told the girl's arm that I had known other women.

From one who was not a great deal older than the girl who had lent me the arm but far more mature in her experience of men, I had heard that fingertips thus hidden by nails were often acutely sensitive. One became used to touching things not with the fingertips but with the nails, and the fingertips therefore tickled when something came against them.

I had shown astonishment at this discovery, and she had gone

※ 110 ※

on: "You're, say, cooking—or eating—and something touches your fingers, and you find yourself hunching your shoulders, it seems so dirty."

Was it the food that seemed unclean, or the tip of the nail? Whatever touched her fingers made her writhe with its uncleanness. Her own cleanness would leave behind a drop of tragic dew, there under the long shadow of the nail. One could not assume that for each of the ten fingers there would be a separate drop of dew.

It was natural that I should want all the more to touch those fingertips, but I held myself back. My solitude held me back. She was a woman on whose body few tender spots could be expected to remain.

And on the body of the girl who had lent me the arm they would be beyond counting. Perhaps, toying with the fingertips of such a girl, I would feel not guilt but affection. But she had not lent me the arm for such mischief. I must not make a comedy of her gesture.

"The window." I noticed not that the window itself was open but that the curtain was undrawn.

"Will anything look in?" asked the girl's arm.

"Some man or woman. Nothing else."

"Nothing human would see me. If anything it would be a self. Yours."

"Self? What is that? Where is it?"

"Far away," said the arm, as if singing in consolation. "People walk around looking for selves, far away."

"And do they come upon them?"

"Far away," said the arm once more.

It seemed to me that the arm and the girl herself were an infinity apart. Would the arm be able to return to the girl, so far away?

Would I be able to take it back, so far away? The arm lay peace⁄fully trusting me; and would the girl be sleeping in the same peaceful confidence? Would there not be harshness, a nightmare? Had she not seemed to be fighting back tears when she parted with it? The arm was now in my room, which the girl herself had not visited.

The dampness clouded the window, like a toad's belly stretched over it. The fog seemed to withhold rain in mid⁄air, and the night outside the window lost distance, even while it was wrapped in limitless distance. There were no roofs to be seen, no horns to be heard.

"I'll close the window," I said, reaching for the curtain. It too was damp. My face loomed up in the window, younger than my thirty⁄three years. I did not hesitate to pull the curtain, how⁄ever. My face disappeared.

Suddenly a remembered window. On the ninth floor of a hotel, two little girls in wide red skirts were playing in the window. Very similar children in similar clothes, perhaps twins, Occidentals. They pounded at the glass, pushing it with their shoulders and shoving at each other. Their mother knitted, her back to the window. If the large pane were to have broken or come loose, they would have fallen from the ninth floor. It was only I who thought them in danger. Their mother was quite unconcerned. The glass was in fact so solid that there was no danger.

"It's beautiful," said the arm on the bed as I turned from the window. Perhaps she was speaking of the curtain, in the same flowered pattern as the bed cover.

"Oh? But it's faded from the sun and almost ready to go." I sat down on the bed and took the arm on my knee. "This is what is beautiful. More beautiful than anything."

Taking the palm of the hand in my own right palm, and the shoulder in my left hand, I flexed the elbow, and then again.

"Behave yourself," said the arm, as if smiling softly. "Having fun?"

"Not in the least."

A smile did come over the arm, crossing it like light. It was exactly the fresh smile on the girl's cheek.

I knew the smile. Elbows on the table, she would fold her hands loosely and rest her chin or cheek on them. The pose should have been inelegant in a young girl; but there was about it a lightly engaging quality that made expressions like "elbows on the table" seem inappropriate. The roundness of the shoulders, the fingers, the chin, the cheeks, the ears, the long, slender neck, the hair, all came together in a single harmonious movement. Using knife and fork deftly, first and little fingers bent, she would raise them ever so slightly from time to time. Food would pass the small lips and she would swallow—I had before me less a person at dinner than an inviting music of hands and face and throat. The light of her smile flowed across the skin of her arm.

The arm seemed to smile because, as I flexed it, very gentle waves passed over the firm, delicate muscles, to send waves of light and shadow over the smooth skin. Earlier, when I had touched the fingertips under the long nails, the light passing over the arm as the elbow bent had caught my eye. It was that, and not any impulse toward mischief, that had made me bend and unbend her arm. I stopped, and gazed at it as it lay stretched out on my knee. Fresh lights and shadows were still passing over it.

"You ask if I'm having fun. You realize that I have permission to change you for my own arm?"

"I do."

"Somehow I'm afraid to."

"Oh?"

"May I?"

"Please."

I heard the permission granted, and wondered whether I could accept it. "Say it again. Say 'please.'"

"Please, please."

I remembered. It was like the voice of a woman who had decided to give herself to me, one not as beautiful as the girl who had lent me the arm. Perhaps there was something a little strange about her.

"Please," she had said, gazing at me. I had put my fingers to her eyelids and closed them. Her voice was trembling. "'Jesus wept. Then said the Jews, Behold how he loved her!'"

"Her" was a mistake for "him." It was the story of the dead Lazarus. Perhaps, herself a woman, she had remembered it wrong, perhaps she had made the substitution intentionally.

The words, so inappropriate to the scene, had shaken me. I gazed at her, wondering if tears would start from the closed eyes.

She opened them and raised her shoulders. I pushed her down with my arm.

"You're hurting me!" She put her hand to the back of her head.

There was a small spot of blood on the white pillow. Parting her hair, I put my lips to the drop of blood swelling on her head.

"It doesn't matter." She took out all her hairpins. "I bleed easily. At the slightest touch."

A hairpin had pierced her skin. A shudder seemed about to pass through her shoulders, but she controlled herself.

Although I think I understand how a woman feels when she gives herself to a man, there is still something unexplained about the act. What is it to her? Why should she wish to do it, why should she take the initiative? I could never really accept the surrender, even knowing that the body of every woman was made for it. Even now, old as I am, it seems strange. And the ways in which various women go about it: unlike if you wish, or similar perhaps, or even identical. Is that not strange? Perhaps the strangeness I find in it all is the curiosity of a younger man, perhaps the despair of one advanced in years. Or perhaps some spiritual debility I suffer from.

Her anguish was not common to all women in the act of surrender. And it was with her only the one time. The silver thread was cut, the golden bowl destroyed.

"Please," the arm had said, and so reminded me of the other girl; but were the two voices in fact similar? Had they not sounded alike because the words were the same? Had the arm acquired independence in this measure of the body from which it was separated? And were the words not the act of giving itself up, of being ready for anything, without restraint or responsibility or remorse? It seemed to me that if I were to accept the invitation and change the arm for my own I would be bringing untold pain to the girl.

I gazed at the arm on my knee. There was a shadow at the inside of the elbow. It seemed that I might be able to suck it in. I pressed it to my lips, to gather in the shadow.

"It tickles. Do behave yourself." The arm was around my neck, avoiding my lips.

"Just when I was having a good drink."

"And what were you drinking?"

I did not answer.

"What were you drinking?"

"The smell of light? Of skin."

The fog seemed thicker; even the magnolia leaves seemed wet. What other warnings would issue from the radio? I started toward my table radio and stopped. To listen to it with the arm around my neck seemed altogether too much. But I suspected I would hear something like this: because of the wet branches and their own wet feet and wings, small birds have fallen to the ground and cannot fly. Automobiles passing through parks should take care not to run over them. And if a warm wind comes up, the fog will perhaps change color. Strange-colored fogs are noxious. Listeners should therefore lock their doors if the fog should turn pink or purple.

"Change color?" I muttered. "Turn pink or purple?"

I pulled at the curtain and looked out. The fog seemed to press down with an empty weight. Was it because of the wind that a thin darkness seemed to be moving about, different from the usual black of night? The thickness of the fog seemed infinite, and yet beyond it something fearsome writhed and coiled.

I remembered that earlier, as I was coming home with the borrowed arm, the head and tail beams of the car driven by the woman in vermilion had come up indistinctly in the fog. A great, blurred sphere of faint purple now seemed to come toward me. I hastily pulled away from the curtain.

"Let's go to bed. Us too."

It seemed as if no one else in the world would be up. To be up was terror.

Taking the arm from my neck and putting it on the table, I changed into a fresh night-kimono, a cotton print. The arm watched me change. I was shy at being watched. Never before had a woman watched me undress in my room.

The arm in my own, I got into bed. I lay facing it, and brought it lightly to my chest. It lay quiet.

Intermittently I could hear a faint sound as of rain, a very light sound, as if the fog had not turned to rain but were itself forming drops. The fingers clasped in my hand beneath the blanket grew warmer; and it gave me the quietest of sensations, the fact that they had not warmed to my own temperature.

"Are you asleep?"

"No," replied the arm.

"You were so quiet, I thought you might be asleep."

"What do you want me to do?"

Opening my kimono, I brought the arm to my chest. The difference in warmth sank in. In the somehow sultry, somehow chilly night, the smoothness of the skin was pleasant.

The lights were still on. I had forgotten to turn them out as I went to bed.

"The lights." I got up, and the arm fell from my chest.

I hastened to pick it up. "Will you turn out the lights?" I started toward the door. "Do you sleep in the dark? Or with lights on?"

The arm did not answer. It would surely know. Why had it not answered? I did not know the girl's nocturnal practices. I compared the two pictures, of her asleep in the dark and with the lights on. I decided that tonight, without her arm, she would have them on. Somehow I too wanted them on. I wanted to gaze at the arm. I wanted to stay awake and watch the arm after it had gone to sleep. But the fingers stretched to turn off the switch by the door.

I went back and lay down in the darkness, the arm by my chest. I lay there silently, waiting for it to go to sleep. Whether dissatisfied or afraid of the dark, the hand lay open at my side, and presently the five fingers were climbing my chest. The elbow bent of its own accord, and the arm embraced me.

There was a delicate pulse at the girl's wrist. It lay over my heart, so that the two pulses sounded against each other. Hers was at first somewhat slower than mine, then they were together. And then I could feel only mine. I did not know which was faster, which slower.

Perhaps this identity of pulse and heartbeat was for a brief period when I might try to exchange the arm for my own. Or had it gone to sleep? I had once heard a woman say that women were less happy in the throes of ecstasy than sleeping peacefully beside their men; but never before had a woman slept beside me as peacefully as this arm.

I was conscious of my beating heart because of the pulsation above it. Between one beat and the next, something sped far away and sped back again. As I listened to the beating, the distance seemed to increase. And however far the something went, however infinitely far, it met nothing at its destination. The next beat summoned it back. I should have been afraid, and was not. Yet I groped for the switch beside my pillow.

Before turning it on, I quietly rolled back the blanket. The arm slept on, unaware of what was happening. A gentle band of faintest white encircled my naked chest, seeming to rise from the flesh itself, like the glow before the dawning of a tiny, warm sun.

I turned on the light. I put my hands to the fingers and shoulder and pulled the arm straight. I turned it quietly in my hands, gazing at the play of light and shadow, from the roundness at the shoulder over the narrowing and swelling of the forearm, the narrowing again at the gentle roundness of the elbow, the faint depression inside the elbow, the narrowing roundness to the wrist, the palm and back of the band, and on to the fingers.

"I'll have it." I was not conscious of muttering the words. In a trance, I removed my right arm and substituted the girl's.

There was a slight gasp—whether from the arm or from me I could not tell—and a spasm at my shoulder. So I knew of the change.

The girl's arm—mine now—was trembling and reaching for the air. Bending it, I brought it close to my mouth.

"Does it hurt? Do you hurt?"

"No. Not at all. Not at all." The words were fitful.

A shudder went through me like lightning. I had the fingers in my mouth.

Somehow I spoke my happiness, but the girl's fingers were at my tongue, and whatever it was I spoke did not form into words.

"Please. It's all right," the arm replied. The trembling stopped. "I was told you could. And yet—"

I noticed something. I could feel the girl's fingers in my mouth, but the fingers of her right hand, now those of my own right hand, could not feel my lips or teeth. In panic I shook my right arm and could not feel the shaking. There was a break, a stop, between arm and shoulder.

"The blood doesn't go," I blurted out. "Does it or doesn't it?"

For the first time I was swept by fear. I rose up in bed. My own arm had fallen beside me. Separated from me, it was an unsightly object. But more important—would not the pulse have stopped? The girl's arm was warm and pulsing; my own looked as if it were growing stiff and cold. With the girl's, I grasped my own right arm. I grasped it, but there was no sensation.

"Is there a pulse?" I asked the arm. "Is it cold?"

"A little. Just a little colder than I am. I've gotten very warm." There was something especially womanly in the cadence. Now that the arm was fastened to my shoulder and made my own, it seemed womanly as it had not before.

"The pulse hasn't stopped?"

"You should be more trusting."

"Of what?"

"You changed your arm for mine, didn't you?"

"Is the blood flowing?"

"'Woman, whom seekest thou?' You know the passage?"

"'Woman, why weepest thou? Whom seekest thou?'"

"Very often when I'm dreaming and wake up in the night I whisper it to myself."

This time of course the "I" would be the owner of the winsome arm at my shoulder. The words from the Bible were as if spoken by an eternal voice, in an eternal place.

"Will she have trouble sleeping?" I too spoke of the girl herself. "Will she be having a nightmare? It's a fog for herds of nightmares to wander in. But the dampness will make even demons cough."

"To keep you from hearing them." The girl's arm, my own still in its hand, covered my right ear.

It was now my own right arm, but the motion seemed to have come not of my volition but of its own, from its heart. Yet the separation was by no means so complete.

"The pulse. The sound of the pulse."

I heard the pulse of my own right arm. The girl's arm had come to my ear with my own arm in its hand, and my own wrist was at my ear. My arm was warm—as the girl's arm had said, just perceptibly cooler than her fingers and my ear.

"I'll keep away the devils." Mischievously, gently, the long, delicate nail of her little finger stirred in my ear. I shook my head. My left hand—mine from the start—took my right wrist—actually the girl's. As I threw my head back, I caught sight of the girl's little finger.

Four fingers of her hand were grasping the arm I had taken from my right shoulder. The little finger alone—shall we say that it alone was allowed to play free?—was bent toward the back of the hand. The tip of the nail touched my right arm lightly. The finger was bent in a position possible only to a girl's supple hand, out of the question for a stiff-jointed man like me. From its base it rose at right angles. At the first joint it bent in another right angle, and at the next in yet another. It thus traced a square, the fourth side formed by the ring finger.

It formed a rectangular window at the level of my eye. Or rather a peep-hole, or an eyeglass, much too small for a window; but somehow I thought of a window. The sort of window a violet might look out through. The window of the little finger, the finger-rimmed eyeglass, so white that it gave off a faint glow—I brought it nearer my eye. I closed the other eye.

"A peep show?" asked the arm. "And what do you see?"

"My dusky old room. Its five lights." Before I had finished the sentence I was almost shouting. "No, no! I see it!"

"And what do you see?"

"It's gone."

"And what did you see?"

"A color. A blur of purple. And inside it little circles, little beads of red and gold, whirling around and around."

"You're tired." The girl's arm put down my right arm, and her fingers gently stroked my eyelids.

"Were the beads of gold and red spinning around in a huge cogwheel? Did I see something in the cogwheel, something that came and went?"

I did not know whether I had actually seen something there or only seemed to—a fleeting illusion, not to stay in the memory. I could not remember what it might have been.

"Was it an illusion you wanted to show me?"

"No. I came to erase it."

"Of days gone by. Of longing and sadness."

On my eyelids the movement of her fingers stopped.

I asked an unexpected question. "When you let down your hair does it cover your shoulders?"

"It does. I wash it in hot water, but afterward—a special quirk of mine, maybe—I pour cold water over it. I like the feel of cold hair against my shoulders and arms, and against my breasts too."

It would of course be the girl again. Her breasts had never been touched by a man, and no doubt she would have had difficulty describing the feel of the cold, wet hair against them. Had the arm, separated from the body, been separated too from the shyness and the reserve?

Quietly I took in my left hand the gentle roundness at the shoulder, now my own. It seemed to me that I had in my hand the roundness, not yet large, of her breasts. The roundness of the shoulder became the soft roundness of breasts.

Her hand lay gently on my eyelids. The fingers and the hand clung softly and sank through, and the underside of the eyelids seemed to warm at the touch. The warmth sank into my eyes.

"The blood is going now," I said quietly. "It is going."

It was not a cry of surprise as when I had noticed that my arm was changed for hers. There was no shuddering and no spasm, in the girl's arm or my shoulder. When had my blood begun to flow through the arm, her blood through me? When had the break at the shoulder disappeared? The clean blood of the girl was now, this very moment, flowing through me; but would there not be unpleasantness when the arm was returned to the girl, this dirty male blood flowing through it? What if it would not attach itself to her shoulder?

"No such betrayal," I muttered.

"It will be all right," whispered the arm.

There was no dramatic awareness that between the arm and my shoulder the blood came and went. My left hand, enfolding my right shoulder, and the shoulder itself, now mine, had a natural understanding of the fact. They had come to know it. The knowledge pulled them down into slumber.

I slept.

I floated on a great wave. It was the encompassing fog turned a faint purple, and there were pale green ripples at the spot where I floated on the great wave, and there alone. The dank solitude of my room was gone. My left hand seemed to rest lightly on the girl's right arm. It seemed that her fingers held magnolia stamens. I could not see them, but I could smell them. We had thrown them away—and when and how had she gathered them up again? The white petals, but a day old, had not yet fallen; why then the stamens? The automobile of the woman in vermilion slid by, drawing a great circle with me at the center. It seemed to watch over our sleep, the arm's and mine.

Our sleep was probably light, but I had never before known sleep so warm, so sweet. A restless sleeper, I had never before been blessed with the sleep of a child.

The long, narrow, delicate nail scratched gently at the palm of my hand, and the slight touch made my sleep deeper. I disappeared.

I awoke screaming. I almost fell out of bed, and staggered three or four steps.

I had awakened to the touch of something repulsive. It was my right arm.

Steadying myself, I looked down at the arm on the bed. I caught my breath, my heart raced, my whole body trembled. I saw the arm in one instant, and the next I had torn the girl's from my shoulder and put back my own. The act was like murder upon a sudden, diabolic impulse.

I knelt by the bed, my chest against it, and rubbed at my insane heart with my restored hand. As the beating slowed down a sadness welled up from deeper than the deepest inside me.

"Where is her arm?" I raised my head.

It lay at the foot of the bed, flung palm up into the heap of the blanket. The outstretched fingers did not move. The arm was faintly white in the dim light.

Crying out in alarm I swept it up and held it tight to my chest. I embraced it as one would a small child from whom life was going. I brought the fingers to my lips. If the dew of woman would but come from between the long nails and the fingertips!

*Of Birds
and Beasts*

禽獸

Of Birds and Beasts

A chirping of birds broke in upon his daydream.

On a dilapidated old truck was a cage that might have been for a criminal on the kabuki stage, though it was two or three times larger.

The man's taxi seemed to have made its way into a funeral procession. The number "23" was pasted on the windshield of the car following, beside the driver's face. The man looked out. They were passing a Zen temple, the stone before which bore the inscription: "Historical Landmark: The Grave of Dazai Shundai."[1] On the gate was pasted a notice that there was to be a funeral.

They were going down a slope. At the foot of it was an inter-section with a policeman directing traffic. Some thirty cars were lined up before it, threatening a jam. He gazed at the cage of birds to be released at the funeral. He was growing impatient.

---

1. Confucian scholar, 1680–1747.

"What time is it?" he asked the maid, a small girl sitting deferentially beside him, a basket of flowers carefully upright in her lap. It was not to be expected that she would have a watch.

"A quarter to seven," the driver answered in her place. "This clock is six or seven minutes slow."

The sunset was still bright in the summer sky. The scent of the roses in the basket was strong. An oppressive scent came from some June blossom in the temple garden.

"We'll be late. Can't you hurry?"

"There's nothing I can do till they've passed in the other lane. What's happening at Hibiya Hall?" The driver was probably thinking of a return fare.

"A dance recital."

"Oh? How long do you suppose it will take to let all those birds go?"

"I imagine it's bad luck to meet a funeral along the way."

There was a loud fluttering of wings. The truck was moving.

"No, it's good luck. They say it's the best luck in the world." As if to give his words emphasis, the driver slipped into the right lane and briskly passed the procession.

"That's strange," laughed the man. "You'd think the opposite." Yet it was to be expected that people should be in the habit of so thinking.

It was strange to be concerned about such things on his way to Chikako's recital. If he wanted to look for bad omens, the fact that they had left two corpses unburied at home should be worse luck than meeting a funeral.

"Get rid of those birds when we get back tonight," he said, almost spitting out the words. "They will still be in the closet upstairs."

It was already a week since the pair of golden-crowned kinglets had died. He had not taken the trouble to dispose of the bodies, but had left them, still in the cage, in the closet at the head of the stairs. They were so used to the corpses of small birds, he and the maid, that they still had not bothered to throw these away, even though they took cushions from under the cage whenever some one came calling.

Along with certain varieties of titmouse and wren and chat, the golden-crowned kinglet is the smallest of caged birds. Olive above and a pale yellow-brown below, it has a brownish neck and two white stripes at the wings. The tips of the pinion feathers are yellow. At the crown of the head is a thick ring of black enclosing a ring of yellow. When the feathers are ruffled the yellow stands out like a single chrysanthemum. In the male it shades off to a deep orange. The round eyes have a certain puckish charm, and there is exuberance in the way the bird has of crawling around the top of its cage. All in all, a most winning and elegant bird.

Since the dealer had brought them at night, the man immediately put the cage away in the dusky recesses of the house altar. Glancing at it somewhat later, he saw that the birds were very beautiful in sleep. Each had its head in the other's feathers, and the two were like a ball of yarn, so close that it was impossible to distinguish one from the other.

Nearing forty, he felt a youthful warmth flow over him, and stood on the table gazing on and on at the altar.

Would there not, he wondered, in some country somewhere, be a pair of young people, in love for the first time, sleeping even thus? He wanted to share the sight, but he did not call the maid.

From the next day, he had the kinglets on the table, to look at as he ate. Even when he had a guest, he had birds and animals with him. Not really listening to what the guest was saying, he would put a bit of feed on his finger and be intent upon training a robin chick; or, a shiba dog on his knee, he would be assiduously squashing fleas.

"I like shibas. They have something of the fatalist in them. You have one on your knee like this, or you put him off in a corner, and he'll stay there without moving for half a day."

And often he would not look at the guest until he got up to leave.

In the summer he kept carp and scarlet minnows in a glass bowl on the parlor table.

"Maybe it's because I'm getting old. I don't like seeing men any more. I don't like men. I get tired the first minute. It has to be a woman, when you're eating, when you're traveling."

"You ought to get married."

"That wouldn't do either. I like mean women. The best way is to know she's a mean one, and go on seeing her as if you hadn't noticed. That's the kind I like for a maid, too."

"And that's why you keep animals?"

"It's different with animals. I have to have something living and moving beside me." Speaking half to himself, he would forget about the guest as he gazed at the carp of various colors and saw how the light on their scales changed as they moved about, and meditated upon the subtle world of light in this narrow expanse of water.

When the dealer had a new bird, he would bring it around unsolicited. The man sometimes had thirty varieties in his study.

"Not another bird!" the maid would complain.

"You should be glad. It's not much of a price to pay to keep me happy for four or five days."

"But you have that solemn expression on your face and you stare at them so."

"It makes you uncomfortable? You think I'm losing my mind? The place is too quiet?"

But for him life was filled with a young freshness for several days after a new bird came. He felt in it the blessings of the universe. Perhaps it was a failing on his part, but he was unable to feel anything of the sort in a human being. And it was easier to see the wonders of creation in a moving bird than in motionless shells and flowers. The little creatures, even when caged, gave forth the joy of life.

It was particularly so with the lively pair of kinglets.

About a month after their arrival, one of the birds flew out as he was feeding them. The maid was flustered, and the bird flew to a camphor tree above the shed. A morning frost was on the leaves of the camphor. The two birds, one in the cage and one outside, called to each other in high, tense voices. He put the cage on the roof of the shed, and birdlime on a stick beside it. The birds called with increasing desperation, but the escaped bird apparently flew off about noon. The pair had come from the mountains behind Nikkō.

The bird left behind was a female. Remembering the pair asleep, he importuned his dealer for a male. He went the rounds of dealers, but with no luck. Finally his dealer got him another pair from the country. He said he wanted only the male.

"They came as a pair. And there would be no point in keeping a single one. I'll let you have the female for nothing."

"But will the three of them get along?"

"Probably. Put the cages together for four or five days and they'll get used to each other."

But, like a child with a new toy, he could not wait. As soon as the dealer had left he put the two new birds in with the old one. The commotion was worse than he had expected. The two new birds, refusing the perch, slapped from side to side of the cage. The old bird stood motionless on the floor, looking up in terror at the new ones. The new ones called to each other, a married pair to whom disaster had come. The throbbing of the three frightened breasts was violent. He put the cage in the closet. The pair came together, calling out to each other, and the single bird kept timidly to itself.

This would not do. He separated them, but then was overcome with pity for the lone female. He put it in with the new male. The male called out to the mate it was separated from, and did not take to the other; but in the course of time they were sleeping close together. When he put the three together the next evening the commotion was not as the day before. The three of them slept in one ball, two heads from either side in the feathers of the third. He went to sleep with the cage at his pillow.

But when he awoke the next morning two were sleeping like a warm ball of yarn. The third lay dead under the perch, its wings half outstretched, its legs taut, its eyes half open. As if it would not do to have the others see the corpse, he took it out and, without telling the maid, threw it in the garbage box. A horrible kind of murder, he thought.

Which had died, he wondered, gazing at the cage. Contrary to what he would have expected, the survivor seemed to be the old female. His affection was greater for the old one. Perhaps favoritism made him think the old one the survivor. He lived without a family, and the favoritism upset him.

"If you are going to make such distinctions, why live with birds and animals? There is a very good object for them known as a human being."

Golden-crowned kinglets are held to be weak, quick to die; but his pair was very healthy.

He bought a baby shrike taken by a poacher, and it was the beginning: the season was at hand when he would not be able to go out for having to feed new chicks down from the moun- tains. Wistaria petals fell on the water when he took the tub out to the veranda to give the birds their baths.

As he was listening to the flapping of wings against the water and cleaning out the cages, he heard children's voices beyond the fence. They seemed to be awaiting the death of some small animal. He pulled himself to the top of the fence, thinking that one of his wirehair puppies might have strayed from the garden. It was a skylark chick. Not yet able to stand up, it was flounder- ing about in the garbage heap. The idea came to him that he might take it in.

"What's happened?"

"The house over there." A primary-school boy pointed toward a green house with poisonous-looking paulownias in front of it. "They threw it away. It'll die, won't it."

"Yes, it will die," he said coldly, leaving the fence.

The family in the green house kept three or four skylarks. They had probably discarded one that would not be a singer. The impulse toward mercy quickly left him: there was no point in taking in a bird that had been discarded as so much garbage.

There are birds among the very young of which it is impossible to distinguish male from female. Dealers bring whole nests down from the mountains, and throw away the females as soon as they can recognize them. The female does not sing and will not sell. Love of birds and animals comes to be a quest for superior ones, and so cruelty takes root. It was his nature to want any pet animal as soon as he saw it, but he knew from experience that such easy affection was in fact a lack of affection, and that it brought slackening in the rhythm of his life. And so, however fine an animal it might be, however earnestly he might be asked to take it, he would refuse if it had been raised by someone else.

All alone, he came to his arbitrary conclusion: he did not like people. Husbands and wives, parents and children, brothers and sisters: the bonds were not easily cut even with the most unsatisfactory of people. One had to be resigned to living with them. And everyone possessed what is called an ego.

There was, on the other hand, a certain sad purity in making playthings of the lives and the habits of animals, and, deciding upon an ideal form, breeding toward it in a manner artificial and distorted: there was in it a godlike newness. Smiling a sardonic smile, he excused them as symbols of the tragedy of the universe and of man, these animal lovers who tormented animals, ever striving toward a purer and purer breed.

One evening the preceding November a kennel keeper who looked like a shriveled orange because of a kidney ailment or something of the sort, came to see him.

"A terrible thing. I let her off the leash when we got to the park, and I lost her in the fog for no more than a minute, and some cur was on her. I pulled her away and kicked her and kicked her until she couldn't stand up. I don't see how it could take—but it has a way of taking just when you don't want it to."

"And you're supposed to be a professional."

"Yes, I can't tell anyone, that's how embarrassing it is. Damned bitch—in just a few seconds she lost me four or five hundred yen."[1] His yellow lips were twitching.

The proud Doberman was slinking along with its head down. It looked timorously up at the kidney patient. The fog came pouring in.

---

1. About a hundred dollars.

The dog was to be sold through the man's good offices. It would be to his discredit, he insisted, if, once sold, it were to have a mongrel litter; but some time later, evidently pressed for money, the kennel man sold the dog without letting him know. Some two or three days afterwards the buyer came to him with the dog. The day after the purchase it had had a stillborn litter.

"The maid heard it whining and opened the shutter, and it was in under the veranda eating a puppy. She was surprised and a little afraid and couldn't see very well in the dark. We don't know how many there were, but she thought it was the last one that was being eaten. We called the veterinary right away, and he said that no kennel should sell a pregnant dog. Some mongrel must have gotten at her and the kennel man had kicked and beaten the life out of her. It was not a normal birth, he said, and maybe she had gotten into the habit of eating her puppies. I ought to take her back. We're all furious. A terrible thing to do to an animal."

"Let me see," he said nonchalantly, lifting the dog and feeling its nipples. "She's raised puppies before. She started eating them because they were dead." He spoke with indifference, though he too was angry and sorry.

There had been mongrels born at his house.

Even on a trip he could not share a room with a man, and he disliked having men stay overnight in his house and did not keep a houseboy; and, though the fact had nothing to do with the way men affected him, he kept only bitches. Unless a male dog was really superior, it could not pass as a stud. Such a dog was expensive, and had to be advertised like a movie actor, and fluctuations in its career were violent. One got caught up in competing import trades, it was like gambling. He had once gone to a kennel and been shown a Japanese terrier famous as a stud. It lay all day on a quilt upstairs, and apparently assumed that when it was brought down a female had come. It was like a well-trained prostitute. Because the hair was short, the unusually well-developed organ was the more conspicuous. Even he turned away in discomfort.

But it was not because of distaste for such matters that he did not keep males. His greatest delight was in delivering and rearing puppies.

It was an unusual Boston terrier. It would dig its way under the fence, or gnaw its way through the bamboo. He had tied it up when it was in heat, but it had eaten through the cord and run out, and the puppies would be mongrels. When the maid woke him he got out of bed with the professional mien of a doctor.

"Bring scissors and cotton. And cut up the straw." It was the straw around the saké keg.

The garden had a gentle newness where it was bathed in the sun of early winter. The dog lay in the sun, a bag like an egg-plant beginning to come from its belly. It made the merest gesture of wagging its tail, and looked pleadingly up at him; and suddenly he felt something like a twinge of compunction.

This had been its first heat, and it was not yet fully grown. The look in its eyes was of having no sense of what birth meant.

"What is happening to me? I don't know what it is, but I don't like it. What am I to do?" The dog seemed shy and embarrassed, but at the same time naive, and willing to leave everything to him, as if taking no responsibility for what it was doing.

He remembered the Chikako of ten years before. Her face when she had sold herself to him had been like the dog's.

"Is it true that you lose feeling when you're in this business?"

"Well it does happen, but if you find a man you like—and

you can't exactly call it business when you have two or three regular men."

"I like you."

"And even so it's no good?"

"No, not that."

"Oh?"

"When I get married, will he know?"

"Yes."

"How should I do it?"

"How did you do it?"

"How was it with your wife?"

"How was it, I wonder."

"Tell me."

"I have no wife." He gazed into her serious face.

"It bothered me because it looked like her," he said to himself as he moved the dog to the littering box.

The first puppy, in a caul, was born immediately. The mother did not know what to do with it. He opened the caul with the scissors and cut the cord. The second caul was a large one, and the two puppies, in a muddy green liquid, seemed to be dead. He quickly wrapped them in a newspaper. Three more were born, all in cauls. The seventh and last one was moving in its caul, but seemed shriveled and weak. He glanced at it, and without opening the caul wrapped it in a newspaper.

"Throw them away somewhere. In the West they weed out puppies, kill the ones that aren't good. They get better dogs that way. We sentimental Japanese aren't up to it. Give her a raw egg or something."

He washed his hands and went back to bed. The fresh happiness of the birth of new life flowed over him, and he wanted to go out walking. He had forgotten that he had killed a puppy.

One morning, just when their eyes were opening, he found one of the puppies dead. He put it in his kimono. When he went out for his morning walk he threw it away. Two or three days later another was dead: the mother stirred up straw to make a nest for herself, and the puppies were buried under it. They did not yet have the strength to dig their way out. The mother did not bother to pull them out. Indeed she would lie on the straw under which they were buried. They would die in the night of cold and suffocation. She was like a foolish human mother who suf-focated her baby at her breast.

"Another one's dead." Calmly slipping it into his kimono and whistling for the dogs, he took them for a walk in a nearby park. The terrier scampering joyously about, quite indifferent to the fact that she had just killed a puppy, made him think again of Chikako.

At the age of eighteen, Chikako had been taken off to Harbin by a dabbler in colonial ventures, and there for some three years she had studied dancing under White Russians. The adventurer had apparently failed in everything. With Chikako in the employ of an orchestra that did the rounds of Manchuria, they presently made their way back to Japan. No sooner had they settled down in Tokyo than Chikako left him and married the accompanist who had been with her in Manchuria. She appeared on the stage and had her own recitals.

In those days the man was counted among those who had ties with the world of music; but it was less that he understood music than that he was giving money every month to a certain music magazine. He went to concerts for purposes of exchanging banter with acquaintances. He saw Chikako dance. He was drawn to the savage decadence in her body. It fascinated him to compare her with the Chikako of six or seven years before. What secret could have made her over into such wildness? He wondered why he had not married her.

But that strange power seemed to collapse from about the fourth recital. He rushed to her dressing room, and despite the fact that, still in dancing clothes, she was taking off her makeup, he tugged at her sleeve and led her to a dark corner backstage.

"Take it away." She pushed his hand from her breast. "It hurts when you even touch it."

"What a stupid thing to do."

"But I've always liked children. I've wanted one of my own."

"Do you mean to bring it up? Do you think you can live with your dancing if you go in for womanish things? What can you do with a baby now? You should be more careful."

"There was nothing I could do."

"Don't be a fool. Do you think it's all that easy for an artist? What does your husband say?"

"He's very pleased. He's very proud of it."

He snorted.

"It's good that I can have a baby, after what I used to be."

"You'd better give up dancing."

"I will not." Unprepared for the violence with which she said it, he fell silent.

She did not have a second child. And presently he stopped seeing her with the first. For that reason, possibly, her marriage began to go sour. He heard rumors about it.

Chikako could not have been as careless as the Boston terrier.

He could have saved the puppies if he had tried. He knew perfectly well that he could have prevented the later deaths if after the first one he had cut the straw finer, or put a cloth over it. But the last puppy went the way of the other three. He did not especially want the puppies to die; he did not especially want to keep them alive. His indifference had to do with the fact that they were mongrels.

Sometimes a dog would come up to him on the street. He would talk to it all the way home, he would feed it and give it a place to sleep. It pleased him that a dog should sense warmth in him. But after he came to keep his own dogs he no longer had an eye for mongrels. So it should be with human beings, he said to himself, scorning the families of the world while deriding his own loneliness.

So it was with the skylark. The feelings of pity with which he thought to take it in had quickly vanished. Telling himself that there was no point in saving a piece of garbage, he had left the children to torture it to death.

But in the moment he had been looking at the skylark, the kinglets had been too long in their bath.

In consternation, he took the bathing cage from the water. Both birds lay on the floor like wet rags. When he took them in his hand their legs twitched.

"Good. They're still alive."

In each hand he clutched a little body, cold to the core, the eyes closed, as if quite beyond hope of saving. He warmed them over the brazier, put more charcoal on, and had the maid fan it. Steam came from the feathers. The birds twitched spasmodically. He thought that the shock of the heat burning into them might give them strength to fight death, but he could not stand the heat himself. He spread a towel on the floor of the cage and put the birds on it, and held the cage to the embers. The towel was burned brown. Though one of the birds would occasionally beat its wings and roll over as if snapped by a spring, they could not stand up, and their eyes were still closed. Their feathers were quite dry; but when he took the cage from the fire they showed no sign of coming back to life. The maid went to the house that kept skylarks and was told that ailing birds should be given bitter tea and wrapped in cotton. Wrapping them in absorbent cotton, he took them up in his hands and put their beaks in tea. They drank. When he offered feed they stretched their necks to take it.

"They've come back to life."

What a clean sort of happiness it was. He saw that he had spent four hours saving the birds.

But they fell each time they tried to sit on the perch. It seemed that their toes would not open. Clenched tight, they were hard and stiff, as if they would break like tiny dry twigs.

"Don't you suppose, sir, that you scorched them?" said the maid.

The feet were a dry, brownish color. He had indeed scorched them—but that fact only added to his annoyance. "How could I possibly scorch them when I had them in my hands and on a towel? Go ask the man at the store what to do if they aren't better by tomorrow."

He locked the door of his study and warmed the feet in his mouth. The feel against his tongue was such as to bring tears. Presently the sweat from his hand was warming the feathers. Soaked in his warmth, the feet were softer. He carefully extended a toe that looked as if it might snap off, and curled it around his little finger. Then he put the foot in his mouth again. He took off the perch and transferred the feed to a small sauce dish on the floor of the cage; but the birds still seemed to have difficulty standing and eating.

"The bird man says that you probably did scorch them," said the maid, back from the shop. "He says you should warm their feet in tea. But he says that birds generally pick away at their own feet until they're healed."

It was true. The birds were pecking and tugging at their own feet with the vigor of woodpeckers, as if to say: "What's wrong, feet? Wake up, feet." And they tried with great determination to stand. He wanted to cheer it on, the brightness in the life of these small creatures. They seemed to find it endlessly strange that something should be wrong with a part of them.

He soaked their feet in tea, but his mouth seemed to be more effective.

The birds had been wild, and when he had taken one into his hand there had been a violent pulsing at the breast; but within a day or two after the accident they were quite used to him, and indeed, chirping happily, would take feed while he was holding them. The change made him yet fonder of them.

But his ministrations seemed to have little effect, and he began neglecting them; and on the sixth morning, their clenched feet coated with dung, the two kinglets lay dead, side by side.

There is something particularly fragile and fleeting about the death of a small bird. Most often the corpses are there in the morning, quite unexpectedly.

The first bird to die in his house had been a linnet. In the night a rat pulled out the tails of a pair of linnets, and the cage was spattered with blood. The male died the next day, but the female, her rear parts red as a baboon's, lived on and on. The males who came as mates died one after another. The female finally died of old age.

"Linnets don't seem to do well here. I won't have any more."

He had never liked such birds as linnets, rather to a school-girl's taste. He preferred, in their astringency, birds that took paste in the Japanese manner to birds that took Western-style birdseed. Among songbirds, he disliked canaries and bush warblers and skylarks and the like, birds with bright, showy songs. He had kept linnets all the same, but only because the dealer had given them to him. When one died he would but get a replacement.

With dogs, too, he did not like to have a breed he had kept, say a collie, die out. A man is drawn to a woman like his mother, loves a woman like his first sweetheart, wants to marry a woman like his dead wife. Is it not the same with birds and beasts? He lived with them because he wanted to savor in solitude a more independent kind of arrogance; and he stopped keeping linnets.

The next bird to die was a yellow wagtail. The yellow-green from the abdomen toward the tail, the yellow of the abdomen and breast, and still more the soft, plain lines, reminded him of a delicate bamboo grove. Especially tame, it would happily take food, if it was from his finger, even when it was not hungry, all the while joyously fanning its wings and chirping in a manner most pleasant; and because it would playfully peck at the moles on his face, he let it out of its cage. The result was that it died from too large a meal of crumbs or something of the sort. He thought he would like another, but gave up the idea, and put a Ryūkyū robin, a new bird for him, into the empty cage.

Regrets for the kinglets did not leave him, perhaps because his negligence had been responsible both for overdoing the bath and for wounding the feet. The dealer brought another pair immediately. Small though they might be, this time he did not for a moment leave the tub; and the same thing happened again.

Their eyes were closed and they were shivering when he took the bathing cage from the water; but, able somehow to stand up, they were in considerably better condition than the earlier ones. He would take care not to scorch the feet.

"I've done it again. Light the charcoal." He spoke quietly, with some embarrassment.

"How would it be to let them die, sir?"

It was as if he had been startled from a slumber. "But you remember how it was last time. I can save them with no trouble at all."

"You might save them, but not for long. I thought so last time, with their feet that way. It would have been better to let them die in a hurry."

"But I could save them if I wanted to."

"It would be better to let them die."

"Oh?" He felt a sudden draining away of his strength, as if he might be fainting. He went upstairs to his study, and, putting the cage in the sunlight at the window, absently watched the kinglets die.

He was praying that the sunlight would save them. He was strangely sad. It was as if his own wretchedness lay there exposed to his gaze. He was unable to work at saving them as he had done for the others.

When, finally, they were dead, he took the wet bodies from the cage. He held them for a time in his hand, then put them back into the cage and shoved it into the closet.

He went downstairs. "They're dead," he said nonchalantly to the maid.

Small and weak, golden-crowned kinglets were quick to die. Yet other small birds, titmice and wrens, did well in his house. That he should have killed two pairs in the bath—he thought it fate, as if a linnet, for instance, had trouble living in a house where a linnet had died.

"That's that between me and kinglets," he laughed. Lying down in the breakfast room, he let the puppies tug at his hair. Then, selecting a horned owl from among the sixteen or seventeen cages, he took it up to his study.

When it saw him the owl would open its eyes wide with anger. Turning and turning its half-buried head, it would rattle its beak and hiss. It would eat nothing while he was watching. When he held out a bit of meat, it would snap angrily, and leave it dangling from its beak. He had spent one whole night in a contest of the wills. It would not look at feed while he was there. It would be motionless. But it got hungry as dawn came into the sky. He would hear it sliding along the perch in the direction of the feed. He would look around, and the head would snap up, horns back, eyes narrow, the expression such as to make one wonder whether there could be such evil and cunning in the world; and, hissing venomously, it would pretend that nothing had happened. He would look away. Again he would hear the feet. Their eyes would meet, and again the owl would pull away. Presently the shrike was noisily sounding the happiness of morning.

Far from resenting the owl, he took great comfort from it.

"I've been looking for a maid like this."

"Very self-effacing of you."

Frowning, he looked away.

"Kiki kiki," he called to the shrike beside them.

"Kikikikikikikiki," replied the shrike, its voice shrill as if to send everything fleeing. Though, like the owl, of violent habits, it was fond of feeding from his hand, and it took to him like a pampered little girl. It would call out when he coughed, or when it heard his footsteps coming home. When he let it out of the cage, it would fly to his shoulder or knee, and flutter its wings happily.

He kept it at his pillow as a substitute for an alarm clock. In the morning light it would call out beguilingly when he turned over or moved an arm or rearranged his pillow. It would even answer when he swallowed. And when it noisily set about awakening him, its voice would be bright as a bolt of lightning through the morning of life. When they had called back and forth several times and he was fully awake, it would chirp quietly in imitation of all the other birds.

The shrike was the first to make him feel the happiness of a a new day, and presently other songs would join in. Still in his nightgown, he would put feed on his finger, and the hungry shrike would peck violently at it. He took the violence as a mark of affection.

He seldom spent a night away from home. If he was away for so much as a night he would dream of his birds and beasts, and be awake. Because his habits were so fixed, he would become bored and turn back when he went out by himself to shop or to visit a friend. If he had no other woman companion, he would take the maid with him,

Now, on his way to see Chikako dance, he could not turn back. He had gone to the trouble of bringing the girl and the basket of flowers.

The recital that evening was sponsored by a newspaper. It was a sort of competition among fourteen or fifteen women dancers.

He had not seen her dance in two years. Her dancing had so degenerated that he had to look away. All that was left of the savage strength was a common coquettishness. Form had gone to pieces with the decay of her body.

He took as his excuse, despite the views of the driver, that it was bad luck to have met a funeral, and that it was bad luck too to have dead birds at home, and sent the girl backstage with the flowers. Chikako sent back the message that she wanted to talk to him. Having seen her dance, he disliked the prospect of having a long talk with her. He took advantage of the intermission to go backstage. He pulled up short, and slipped behind the door.

Chikako was being made up by a young man.

On the still, white face, utterly given over to the man, the eyes were closed, the outstretched chin was slightly raised, the lips and the eyebrows and eyelashes had not yet been painted. It was like the face of a lifeless doll, a dead face.

Not quite ten years before he had thought of committing suicide with Chikako. They had had no special reason. He had been in the habit of saying he wanted to die. The thought was but a scum floating upon the solitary life he lived with his animals; and he decided that Chikako, who absently gave herself over to others as if asking that someone bring her hope, who was scarcely alive at all, would be a good companion. Chikako, the expression on her face the usual one, as if she did not know the significance of what she was doing, nodded childishly. She set but one condition.

"They say you kick at your skirt. Tie my legs up tight."

Tying her legs with a thin cord, he was surprised anew at their beauty.

He thought: "They'll say that I died with a beautiful woman."

She lay with her back to him, her eyes calmly closed, her head up. Then she brought her hands together in prayer. He was struck, as by lightning, by the joy of emptiness.

"We are not to die."

He had of course not been of a mind to kill and to die. He did not know whether or not Chikako had been serious. Her face revealed nothing. It was a midsummer afternoon.

Quite taken by surprise, he neither spoke nor thought again of suicide. The knowledge echoed deep in his heart that whatever happened he must treasure this woman.

The face of Chikako given over to the young man made him think of her face as she had lain hands clasped. The thoughts that had been with him since he got into the cab were of that same face. Whenever he thought of Chikako, even at night, she was wrapped in the blinding light of midsummer.

"But why did I slip behind the door?" he muttered to himself as he started back down the hall. A man greeted him cordially. Who might he be? He seemed very excited, whoever he was.

"She *is* good. You see how good she is when she's set off by the others."

He remembered. It was the accompanist whom Chikako had married.

"And how are things?"

"I've been thinking I should come by and say hello. As a matter of fact we were divorced the end of last year. But her dancing does stand out. She *is* good."

In confusion, he said to himself that he must think of something sweet. A certain passage came into his mind.

He had with him the writings of a girl who had died at fifteen. His greatest pleasure these days was in the writings of young boys and girls. Her mother seems to have made up her dead face. After the diary entry for the day of the girl's death she wrote:

"Made up for the very first time: like a bride."

NOTES

For purposes of clarity the translator wishes to include a list of scientific names or descriptions of the plants and animals that are not common in the West. They are given here in the order in which they appear in the text.

"House of the Sleeping Beauties"

page 22, line 20 : *Aoki*; *Aucuba japonica.*
page 48, line 13 : White rhododendron (*Asebi*); *Pieris japonica.*

"Of Birds and Beasts"

page 128, line 31 : Golden-crowned kinglet (*Kikuitadaki,* literally "chrysanthemum crown"); *Regulus regulus Japonensis.*
page 129, line 7 : "certain varieties of titmouse. . . ." Three varieties of titmouse are mentioned in the Japanese text, along with a wren and a chat.
page 130, line 2 : Robin (*Komadori*); *Erithacus akahige.*
Shiba dog; a Japanese breed resembling but smaller than the Akita.
page 143, line 20 : Ryūkyū robin (*Akahige*); *Erithacus komadori komadori.*